Betty

Betty

DAVID DAWN

Library of Congress Control Number:		2014913531
ISBN:	Hardcover	978-1-4990-5656-3
	Softcover	978-1-4990-5657-0
	eBook	978-1-4990-5655-6

This book was printed in the United States of America.

Rev. date: 08/26/2014

To order additional copies of this book, contact:
Xlibris LLC
1-888-795-4274
www.Xlibris.com
Orders@Xlibris.com
634012

CONTENTS

Introduction..7

Chapter # 1   Little Miss Know It All 11

Chapter # 2   Living the Real Life as an Adult................31

Chapter # 3   Making Babies 43

Chapter # 4   Hard Times Raising Children....................51

Chapter # 5   Growing Pains 61

Chapter # 6   The Move to Seattle....................................69

Chapter # 7   The Golden Years 77

INTRODUCTION

T HIS BOOK IS based on a true story of a woman who was raised in the roaring 20's ran away from her home to seek out a new life for her self during the Great Depression. During this time the American public was very critical of women working and mixing with nonwhite races. In 1920 The 19th Amendment to the constitution was passed, giving women the equal right to vote. The industrialist thought that the women's rights movement was over because the women had what they wanted. It was not true in the work place, especially for women of color were the discrimination continued against in virtually every sector of society. The 1930s are an especially interesting period because, although discrimination still existed, the Great Depression took center stage. Living through that period while facing discrimination was especially difficult for many women.

Betty was one of the lucky ones because she was a white woman who stayed away from drugs and the criminal environment. When she was young she made very poor decisions when it came to selecting men and that by it self made living life very hard for her and her family.

Most teenagers who run away from home find out that they have made a mistake. Unfortunately a lot of them was like Betty who had too much pride to go back home. Every teenager has the choice to be either rebellious and self centered or to follow the rules of society. The rebellious ones and their families will suffer by living in a financially deprived environment. Many do not realize that in most of the cases, it is never too late to go back home and finish growing up and become a young adult with the wisdom and knowledge of their parents.

The young people of the 21st century must realize that the technology has really changed the way people do their job, communicate, travel, etc., etc., etc. As far as our social cycles are concerned they are the same. In the world of social cycles only the faces and places change. All of the mental games are still the same. We feel the same, think the same and do the same social actions as our grand parents and, or our ancient ancestors. You do not have to be living in the Great Depression area to have hard times. Just raising a family and meeting the needs of that family will bring hard times and to the week minded a great state of depression.

The Great Depression closed down or slowed down the male dominated industries the hardest. Due to the way society thought the men that had lost their jobs believed that they were failures in society. Men could not work in the stereotyped society industries like the clerical, garment, and servants because these were jobs for ladies only, but the race of the employees changed. The status of people was white men, white ladies, black ladies and black men. This was the way the employment status has always been in our American society between blacks and whites. Married women who started working made the percentage of working women grow by 26% from 1929 to 1940 and it grew during WWII. This is the beginning of women being the bread winners of the family.

This story is geared to helping young adults to become mentally focused on the important aspects of life. One of these aspects is to get them ready to be adults living on their own and be productive citizens. The young people must realize that if they do as they are told by their parents and other responsible adults they will go much farther in life by getting good education. This will lead to a good job and being able to make good money to raise a family better then what their parents did. It is the mission of teenagers to learn their family history and see why their parents had the beliefs and habits that they have. With that knowledge a person can change their own bad habits and cycles that they were taught. Only then a person can turn those cycles in to positive ones that will help them achieve more in life then their parents had. Young people need to start thinking of this not only for their future but for the future of their family. To be able to give their children more than what you had.

Some people say that we are living here for a reason and we will not die until we have full filled our reason for being and Betty believed in this. She raised her kids to be hard working, loving adults and showed them that people can change the negative cycles that are in their lives. Each new day gives a person another chance to continue their fight for changing to be the person who they really want to be.

CHAPTER 1

Little Miss Know It All

PUGET SOUND IS one of the most beautiful bodies of water with it's cities on the water front. The cities are backed up with green rolling hills and two snow capped mountain ranges that reach up to the sky. This story starts in Seattle, largest city in the northwest.

I have a beautiful view. I can see the Space Needle to the north, part of the south end of Queen Ann Hill and the most beautiful of all, a part of Puget Sound. I enjoyed seeing the sailboats float by and the speed boats cut through the water or occasionally the fire boats spraying out their beautiful streams of water in to the air. I have seen a lot of large ships go by along with the ferry boats coming and going. All of this is backed up with the beauty of the snow capped Olympic Mountains on the other side of Puget Sound with their beautiful sun sets showing off the golden clouds year round. It was not a wide view of the mountains because of the buildings lining the street but it still was a great view of the mountains and the sound.

Today started out to be a beautiful sun shine morning. I took a look out of my living room window to see the Olympic Mountains on the other side of Puget Sound. I could see clouds beginning to roll over the Olympic Mountains heading straight for the city. I have seen these clouds several times before and it was a good heavy rain coming our way. I figured I might have enough time to go down to the local café for breakfast.

As I was putting on my coat, I could hear the sound of fire engines sirens going off at the near by fire station. I loved to watch them go up the avenue with their lights flashing. One of the advantages to living in a high rise is sometimes you get a good view and that is what I had. I could see all of the way up 3rd Avenue to the Space Needle and Queen Ann Hill. I had always wanted to be the driver of a fire engine. I always pictured myself driving one as I watched the hook and ladder fire engine, hose fire engine, first aid truck and the fire Chiefs SUV, winding through traffic with their lights and sirens on. It was always a joy to watch. I watched them for at least twenty-five blocks as the fire equipment went out of view.

My stomach soon reminded me of breakfast and I wanted to be back before the rain came, because those clouds looked pretty dark and with them looking like that, it normally meant there is a lot of wind and rain that goes with along with them.

As I was walking to the café, I noticed a young girl who looked about five months pregnant. She was just sitting on the park bench wasting time and then I remembered seeing this young lady in the neighborhood for the last week or two. She reminded me of myself when I was young and dumb.

The closer I got to the café the stronger the wind was getting. You could smell the rain in the air. I was glad to get to the café. I greeted some of the other regulars and Miss Johnston who I befriended my very first day in Seattle. I was lucky to get my favorite seat next to the window. I liked to watch the world go by while eating my meals. I noticed the same young pregnant girl that was at the park walking by the window. She was pulling a big suit case on wheels and she came in to the café to get out of the wind.

The pregnant girl and I had eye to eye contact and I waved to her to come over to me. As the girl approached I asked if she would like to join me at the table. The girl accepted and low and behold the conversation was on. If one of us was not talking the other one was.

Miss Johnston was busy serving other customers. She always had an ear listening to customers conversations. When it was time to order the food the girl said, "I will have only coffee please". Miss Johnston and I knew what was up as we gave each other a knowing look. Miss Johnston said, "Oh no baby girl, now, don't you worry, we are going to fix you up. You just have a look at the menu and I will be right back to take your order."

Sue was the girls' name, she asked me about my life. I looked at her with a strange funny look and said, "To be honest I started out like you. I was like all the teenagers who thought that they were grown enough to handle all of the different types of situations in life. I was a little Miss know it all, but I was one of the lucky ones because I stayed away from drugs and the criminal environment. I did make very poor decisions when it came to selecting men and that by itself made living life very hard for me and my family." I had to tell Sue that it is never too late to go back home. You just need to swallow your pride and be a young adult about it. Go to your parents and admit to them that you were wrong. The grass always looks greener on the other side. This means, once you get to where you wanted to go you will find out that every thing is completely different then what you had thought it would be. I found out that most of the time it turns out to be a lot worse then what you had left.

Miss Johnston walked by with out breaking her stride and she said to Sue, "you need to take heed to what you are being told, baby girl" Sue and I just looked at each other and I had to say to Sue, "you know she is right"

As I look back at it now I wish that I did not run away from home. I had it made and I did not even know it. Sure, I would have had to put up with their racist ways but I knew better. I could have lived any way I wanted after I become of age. I could have had the time to save some money and moved to a place of my own. Getting started would have been a lot easier too, because I would have had their full support. I would have finished high school and most likely would have had a better job because of the high school diploma and the wisdom of being older. "Sue I am just saying that my whole world would have been better, just by staying at home for three or four more years."

"I guess you can say that I was too impatient and just plain spoiled, dumb and hard headed. I was raised in a sheltered life and I had very little to worry about. My Mother had actually spoiled me too much. My mom thought that spoiling me was the answer to keeping every thing under control. She always tried to give me every thing she could with out me having to work for it. Dad always bought me off with money or favors rather than sitting me down and talking to me. I was just like any other spoiled teenager, a know it all. I took advantage of my mom in every way I could, as all kids do in taking every thing to its limit. As a matter of fact I had a lot to learn when it came to living on my own and I was not even close to being ready. I was not educated about the cold hard facts of the real world outside of my home. I had to learn how fast, hard and unforgiving it really is without the shelter of my home and the support of my loving parents."

Mr. Willaims was sitting at the counter having breakfast and heard our conversation. He turned and stated that he was a run away who became a player. He asked if he could put in his two cents? Of course, we both agreed to hear what he had to say. Mr. Williams face went in to a distant stare as he started talking, "Most teenagers who run away from home come to find out that they have made a mistake. Unfortunately a lot of them was like Betty who had too much pride to go back home. They choose to live on the streets in a life of self denial blaming their parents for their immature, selfish and spoiled ways. Most of these girls normally end up having babies and fall in to the criminal world doing what ever they can just to survive. Some of them start hanging around people who make the fast and easy money because a teenager does need a roof over their head, food in their stomach and money to spend. There is a lot more to know when living on the streets than what meets the eye. If you want to be successful at living on the streets you have to have a cold heart and do not trust anyone. You need to think only of yourself. This not a nine to five job, this is a 24-7 job. Most of the people hustling on the streets find themselves in prison, hooked on drugs and being used by others who are stronger. Most teenagers figure they will not get caught only to find out that eventually they will get caught. They do not think about after being prosecuted several times, even for minor offences, they would be creating criminal records that will stay with them forever. When they are in their twenties they finally realize that their records will haunt them when they try to look for jobs or go to school and it could affect their quality of living. They come to realize that creating a criminal record actually makes every thing four times harder to do. A lot of people just give up and stay living in that low life stile, which is the wrong thing to do. You never give up. You must fight four times harder to do the right things in life.

Every teenager has the choice to be either rebellious or self centered or to follow the rules of society. On the average, by the time a person who lives life in the fast lane wakes up, they are ten years behind those who played by societies rules. They will be lucky to have a career at thirty, while the grads or teenagers who stopped living the fast life and got a GED will start in their twenty's. The rebellious ones and their families will suffer by living in a financially deprived environment and the research shows that the odds of your children following your way of life are great. In the cycles of life the odds are great that this type of living will go on for generations. The only way to break the cycle is to know your family history, being honest with yourself and choosing to change the negative things in your life with passion and desire.

Many do not realize that it is never too late to go back home and finish growing up and become a young adult with the wisdom and knowledge of their parents. By doing this they will have a better idea of how to have the patience to deal with the things they really do not want to do. They will learn to know how important it is to follow orders and finish a project. They will be taught how to apply themselves the right way to get and keep a job. All of this is for their own good so they can have a better life when they get on their own".

The young people of today must realize that the technology has really changed the way people do their job, communicate, travel, etc., etc., etc., but, as far as our social cycles are concerned they are the same. We feel the same, think the same and do the same social actions as our grand parents and our ancient ancestors. As the saying goes, "the faces and places change but the game is still the same".

With that being said Mr. William got up from his chair and said, "It has been nice telling the both of you about what I found to be the facts of life. I wish I could stay but I have some things to take care of." As he started walking out he said, "You ladies have a great day." I was impressed with the knowledge of the man.

I had to make a lot of daily sacrifices to raise my children and most teens do not realize the huge sacrifice they must make in order to raise their babies in a well rounded atmosphere. The parent must sacrifice their free time that they have to spend normally with their friends, sleep, relaxation and extra money. Raising a child is a 24-7 job with no pay as far as dollars is concern. The only pay is though there is the satification of seeing your baby being raised right with plenty of love.

Miss Johnston came by to get our orders and of course she had to jump in to the conversation. Girl, let me tell you that she is so right and back in the day every woman across the nation had fought hard to have the choice referring to their reproductive rights. Back in the day the consequences for men was different when it came to sexual relations. As it is today men were not fair in accepting the responsibility for a child. The old double standard stated that men were rewarded for sexual acts and the woman suffered a damaged reputation. Society encouraged men to have sex and women were told' good girls are not to have sex. Men had the right to have sex with their wife with out consent at any time they wish. A man could rape his wife at will and the wife was illegally obligated to have children by their husband. A lot of sexual relationships did result in the woman getting pregnant and she was the one who was left alone with the responsibilities for raising the baby and you two ladies are witness to the fact.

Women like Margaret Sanger fought for many decades in the hope that women could have the right to use contraceptives. In 1960 the birth control pill came out and it was the first time ladies had the choice to stop pregnancy when having sex. The Roman Catholic Church was set against artificial contraceptives. It was a sin in the eyes of the God. Most states were strongly against abortion as well. This lead to an intense fight over the right for ladies to use contraceptives. Many states sided with the church and prohibited the sale of contraceptives even to married couples. In 1965 the Supreme Court ruled that such laws were unconstitional and in the 1970's the courts across the land followed suit. The sexual revolution had started. Young couples started living together before marrage which started a tremendous change in the life style of the American youth. They were also encouraged buy the movie industry with R and X rated movies.

I had to interrupt her in her history lesion and remind her of getting our food. We were starving and I needed more coffee. As Miss Johnston walked away with a little attitude, then she turned and said, "Your food is not ready yet and I am not finished with my story". Miss. Johnston wanted to add that just as ladies had to sacrifice for their babies, they also had to sacrifice for their families and for society. Many states restricted women from property rights, they could not sell property once their husband and father died, they could not make contracts which included wills, they could not control their own earnings and this was the right of the husband or father.

The Great Depression really did affect young single ladies in many different ways. Women were forced to abandon their goals, dreams and expectations that they had planed for themselves. They had to sacrificed marriage, education, independence and children in order to help their families. Women came up with remarkable ways to keep their families afloat during this time. They helped their families get by on less and maximized every opportunity to save money. They bought day old bread and old vegetables and meat that was about to go bad, they used old fabric or blankets to line their coats. They cut up adult clothes to put on their children; parents cut short their children's education and put them to work. Over 80% of young single urban women worked and most of them lived with their families in order to help make ends meet. Any way a person can think of to save money, they did it. In 1932, only three quarters of the people got married compared to the late 1920's and the birth rate declined 24% during the same time.

Even before the 1940's, women of color were affected in different ways and their sacrifice was even greater then the white woman's. Take the Black American woman, for example long before the Great Depression even started she was already at the bottom of the economic ladder. The black woman faced both sexual and racial discrimination in the work place and through out society. Once the depression hit they had to loose their jobs to white women, which caused wide spread unemployment among the black ladies. The black women work force declined 26% as white women moved down the occupational employment ladder. Elite women still enjoyed the good times because in reality when depressions hit the rich get richer and the poor gets poorer. This is due to people selling their belongings to strive and the rich buying it at less then half of its true value.

Then women had to deal with unemployed male relatives who were depressed angered and felt insecure which lead to divorces. During the depression 1.5 million unemployed men left their families. Women had to take care of the family and bring home the money too. Just as the single parent family today. Society and their own families resented the woman if they held a job because the society's structure made people think that the job could have been filled by a man. A lot of the times a woman could find a job as to where a man could not and this were especially true in the black culture. Unemployment has always been high with black men even when the times were good and it is this way today.

The cook called out to Miss. Johnston about the food being ready. Miss Johnston stopped her history lesion and said, "Oh, there is your food. I will be back to tell you ladies more after I serve these people."

Sue said, "I was not aware of the sacrifices the women had to make back in those days, is it true Betty?" I replied, "Of course it is, Miss Johnston knows a lot about the sacrifices of the American women. Look at those pictures on the wall over there they are pictures of Miss Johnston's mother and Grand Mother who was deeply involved in the woman's right movement from the very beginning. They volunteered most of their lives to help over come the injustices of the male dominated society. Lord knows when it comes to woman's rights she knows it all."

Sue said, "Tell me more about your past." I said O.K. and started with, "I traced my family tree all the way back to twenty years after the pilgrims landed. That is when my ancestors came from Holland and England. I was born in an upper middle class family in Philly, in the year of 1919. I was raised in New York. My parents worked hard to maintain the image that they thought was needed to be respected within the neighborhood. It included looking down on other races and believing that they could never bend down to associate with any body who did not meet their standard of society which has always been driven by greed."

When I was being raised it was the time society called the roaring twenties because all the machines were being switched from the steam engines to the gas and electric driven machines. The machine age was soaring and it seem like every thing was new. The whole nation was literally being lit up with lights. They were stringing wires everywhere for electricity. Everything you can think of was being sold on the market from washing machines, ice boxes, sewing machines, spinners on the wheels of cars to the futuristic look of streamlined trains. It seem like every thing was made of chromed from the appliances in the kitchen to the trains, cars and planes. Man kind was on top of the world with science, fashion, machinery, being the supreme race and the head of the family, the bread winner and the only one in the family to wear the pants. Mans ego was on cloud nine.

The big band music was the new sound for that time. My parents like all of the old folk stayed in their own ways they hated the big band music and the type of dancing it produced, which was even more outrageous. It is the same way people my age thought about rock and roll. I did not realize how the cycles of life repeats it's self from generation to generation. I felt the same as my parents did about the kind of music that my children listened to. During my time for raising kids I felt like most of the older folk of that time. We liked the big band music and hated the music of the young folk which was jazz and rock and roll.

I had it made as a child living in the atmosphere of the roaring twenties. Always seeing and hearing about all the new and modern things that were out on the market. I had no Idea that all of this could end. When I ran away from home I was not aware of the state of the union was in a Great Depression.

Miss Johnston came by to check on our orders and to see if we needed any thing else. Every body has what they need and now she has time to jump back in to the conversation. She heard me referring to the 1930s and she went off talking about her grand mother who was deep in to women's rights. She started out with, "the times of the great depression were so bad the employers thought that they could treat their employees any way that they wanted and get away with it, which they did for several years. They did not care bout the working conditions. But they did not take in mind that the women of that time were fearless because they had nothing to loose they were living at the bottom of all of the classes and there was no where to go, but up."

In the early 1930's before the depression the majority of married women had not worked and had to stay at home to take care of their families. Since their men had lost their jobs and could not find a job or find a job that had good pay to raise a family, the wife had to find work. The white married woman had to get out of the house and find her self a job in order to bring in enough money to at least maintain the very basics of life. Half of the state and local governments across the nation made laws that would bar married women from working in government jobs. As a result, public school and transportation systems nationwide began to fire and refuse to hire married women. Banks, insurance companies, public utilities companies, and railways also discriminated against married women in their hiring practices. Also, traditional labor unions, like those associated with the AFL, almost entirely excluded women during the early 1930s. This was due to Congress passing the Federal Economy Act in 1932, which through explicit language excluded a married woman from working in civil service. The media was totally against working mothers. They refused to recognize that the large numbers of married women who entered the Depression-era labor force did so out of the necessity in an effort to save their families from starvation and homelessness.

The white and black women began to organize into local groups that worked to control rent and food prices, to get government relief payments, and to create employment opportunities. They followed in the footsteps of the early 20th century meat and rent strikes in New York. The Unemployed Councils emerged in cities across the country. Women and men in these neighborhood-based groups organized protests of evictions and picketed government relief offices for more unemployment benefits. Housewives' Leagues also emerged in both white and black neighborhoods nationwide.

Leagues of white housewives organized strikes and boycotts on the meat packing industry itself. African-American Housewives' Leagues initiated canvasses, negotiations, and boycotts on the local level to convince neighborhood businesses to hire black employees. The Detroit black women's Housewives' League was founded in 1930 by Fannie Peck, and by 1935, the League had over 10,000 members. Nationwide, these Leagues created 75,000 jobs for African Americans, overcoming racial discrimination and helping some of the devastating effects of the depression. Keep in mind what ever happened to the white race it was always worse for the races of color.

Black women's militant activism and leadership during this oppression helped create the Civil Rights movement of the 20th century. Despite the risk of great personal loss, African-American women have had a long tradition of civil and human rights activism. That tradition lives on today in the experiences and examples of women activists and leaders with the organizational skills and grassroots activism of women like Ella Baker, Septima Clark, Rosa Parks and Fannie Lou Hammer pushed the movement forward to many successes and inspired a new generation of activists like Angela Davis, Marian Wright Edelman, Eleanor Holmes Norton, Maxine Waters and Alice Walker

Some customers came in to eat so Miss. Johnston had to excuse her self. I decided to carry on with my story and I was surprise to see that Sue was all ears. I did not get in to the women's rights movement because I was basically a young open minded, care free, loving righteous kid and the older I got the stronger I became in my beliefs which was just the opposite of my parents. I befriended some black girls and found that all of the things that I was told about other races were a lie. They had the same wants and needs as the white race and they lived their family lives the same too. In my eyes the only thing different was the color of their skin and hair. These black girls came from the same middle class family type living as I did. They were smart, well dressed and they had the same family problems as I did. I found out that what I was told about the black race only went for a few and not the majority of them. I had also found out that the majority of all races have good hard working, law biding people in it. It is just the small amount of negative people of each race which is the negative people of other races that get looked at and harped on. People see the bad things of a race on TV or read it in the papers and actually believe what they see and hear. This is because that is the only source of information for them due to not having actual contact with other races. The racist in the government and organizations use the media knowing that the media is their only contact to out side of their neighborhood, which leads to people really believe in the news that they see and hear. They have even come up with a name for it, which is called stereo typing. It is like the good hard working, law obeying majority of the people of that race does not exist. As I grew older I started to not like the racism of my white friends and their parents which was the same ideas and beliefs as my parents.

My mom and dad were seeing me grow up and they did not want to let go of the little girl that they were used to seeing. They refused to see their little girl changing with the times, along with the music, new ideas and the times of the roaring twenties. My parents wanted to keep me sheltered for as long as possible and as time went on it got worst for me and them. The harder they tried to do this, the more I wanted to see and experience the world that I was sheltered from. At the age of fourteen I was growing in to be a really good looking young lady and the boys at my school did not hide it from me. I really did love my parents but I was being smothered by their old fashion rules that referred to almost every aspect of life. This made it harder for me to see eye to eye with them.

I remember that I wanted to wear my dresses half way up to my knees and start wearing make up and I had the two top buttons loose on my dress. It was the fashion of the times and all of the other girls my age were dressing that way. I remember sneaking around behind my parents back and getting caught some times. This had made things slowly get worse until one day my father caught me with lip stick in my purse. I became rebellious and started smarting off to my father. It hit the fan, o' lord that was it; this was the last straw for my father. He got really mad and started saying a lot of false things about me flirting with the boys and dressing sexy, looking like a street walker with the make up I used. I was disgracing the family running around the neighborhood dressed like that and hanging around them there blacks which leads the people around here to think that we are a family of nigger lovers. He kept on talking about how they did every thing they could for me and how I did not respect them and so on.

Well, for me that was the last straw for me as well and I decide it is time to move on. The last thing I wanted to do was to have their neighbors think that they are nigreo loven white trash. That night I packed my bags and was walking down the road, long before sun rise. As I crossed the street intersections I could feel the cold wind coming from the north and with that feeling I knew that I had to go south.

One block after the other, my feet started hurting with each step. I do not think that I had ever walked so far in my life. I was wearing my Sunday go to meeting shoes and I know that they had never seen so much walking. The pain in my feet told me, "That these shoes were not made for going such long distances." Sue, you are lucky because back in the day we did not have rollers on our suit cases. We had to carry them and my hands and arms started really feeling the weight of my two suit cases which were packed to the brim. I was hard headed like my father and I was determined to go through this.

Soon, I was walking in a daze with only one thing on my mind and that was the highway out of town. I was almost there when I started to notice some boys across the street standing in front of an after hours joint. The, want to be men, had been calling to me for a while and I was so tired of walking that I did not notice the boys till I was directly across the street from them. I just glanced over at them and keep on walking. This offended the boys and they started throwing their beer bottles across the street at me. With each bottle thrown the boys cat calling was getting worst and as the second and third bottle exploded on the wall that I was walking next to. They were yelling bitch, whore and offering me free sex. I started feeling relived because I had walked pass the boys but I can still hear them yelling and a couple more bottles crashed in the street and gutter.

Soon after the boys a car rolls up along side of me and a well dressed white man said, "hey little lady, let me give you a ride to were you are going." I stopped and looked to see who was talking to me. He continued with, "Oh come on I am not like those boys back there. I promise I will not bite." I said no thank you. He replied with, "Okay.

My name is Steve and I would like you to eat breakfast with me, I will buy, the café is just right down the road, come on coffee and eggs is not going to hurt you, please". My feet and my arms were killing me from carrying the heavy luggage. With this in mind I said, "Yes". Steve got out and put my bags in the back seat and closed my door, like a gentleman.

As we were sitting in the café enjoying our breakfast, Steve was asking a lot of questions about me. With me not thinking I answered with them all truthfully, thinking nothing of it. At the end of breakfast I was feeling real good with a full stomach and sipping on some hot coffee. I started thinking that God blessed me with Steve. I even accepted a ride from Steve to the highway.

While driving there, Steve asked me if I wanted to work for him. He said, "That my room and board would be paid for and that I would have every thing I needed." I then asked him, "What type of work I would be doing". He took hold of my hand and said, "All that you would need to do is to go to work on the street for me". I was surprised and before I could say anything he continued with, "not selling your fine body. We would be setting up tricks to get robbed and may be taking numbers or selling a little dope". Steve was smooth and made every thing sound so easy to do. He assured me that with him teaching me there would be nothing to worry about. I wanted to say yes because it sounded too good to be true.

I was scared of breaking the law even though it is the easy life making good money or an easy way out from working a real job that did not pay much. I almost said, "Yes", but I needed to leave this town and this town was Steve's home. So I said, "No" to his offer. We got in the car and started driving to the highway. Steve did not want to take no for an answer so he kept on trying to convince me to join him and the more I said no the more he raised his voice and he stared at me with a crazy look on his face.

Once he knew I was not going to take his offer, he flipped. Steve pulled the car over to the side of the road. Before I could open the car door, Steve grabbed my hair and yanked me closer to him. He looked at me with madness in his eyes and said, "Now bitch you listen to me, I fed you and gave you a ride and now you owe me, where is your money." I tried to explain to Steve and then he pulled real hard on my hair, soooo hard, it felt like it was coming out. I could not stop the tears from running down my cheeks and he kept talking, "Bitch give me your money or I will make you get out there and make me some money, isn't nothen free in life bitch, you better wake up and get for real, who do you think you are messen with". All I could think about was if he pulls a little harder I will loose a lot of hair and then I would have a big bald spot. So I reached in my pocket and gave him all of my savings for the last ten years, it was well over 100 dollars. With a little yank of her hair, Steve said, "You are one lucky little bitch, you're lucky I don't rape you and put your ass out to make me money whoen, now get out of my car". I was lucky that I just had just pulled my hair and took my money because it could have been much worst. He could have kidnaped me, got me hooked on drugs, raped me, make me work the streets for him or worse.

It did not take long for me to walk to the highway and get a ride with a sales man named George. He was not heading due south but the way I was feeling any where but here was good for me. The salesman was a nice man. He said that he was going several hundred miles down the road. I told him about Steve and my life with my parents. George didn't have much to say, but one thing I do remember him saying, "The grass always looks greener on the other side and most of the time it is not greener once you get there". Or in other words it is not going to be easier for me just because I left home. As a matter of fact it is going to be a lot harder. But just like all young know it all's, I had to learn the hard way. George told me to go back home and put up with her parents for a couple more years and at that time I will be a lot more educated about the real world. The things I did not like about my parents were small issues which could be solved by me just talking and really listening to what they have to say. All of the small issues of the past will be big issues in the real world. At the time I did not think much of Georges little speech, most of it went in one ear and out of the other ear.

After driving all day George was pretty tired of driving and he was hungry as well. He told me that he will pay for the dinner but I will have to sleep in the car for the night because he was one horny old man who could not trust his self with me. We had a nice dinner and George took out a pillow and blanket for me to sleep with in the car. The next morning we had breakfast and were back on the road. George should be at his destination by noon to day. We pulled in to town and George said, "Here we are young lady". I thanked him and he replied with, "Really Betty, you should be going back home, every one deserves the right to their own opinion and every parent wants the best for their kids, you have only a couple of years left to be with them, go home". With those words being the last said, George drove off down the road leaving me standing there. I was broke and holding my suit cases in each hand and on top of that, I did not know where I was or where I was going to go. I did not know what to do next, so I decided to just stay where I was and start hitch hiking. Low and be hold, I did not have to wait long when a pickup truck stopped and the lady driver asked me, "How far down the road ya goin". I said, "As far as I can". The lady driver introduced her self as Miss Linda who owned a bed and breakfast in the next little town. With me being my self, I told Miss Linda all about my life and my earlier rides.

Miss. Johnston came to serve us our food and of course she had to jump in to the conversation. She heard me referring to the 1930s and she went off, talking about her grand mother who was deep in to women's rights at that time. Girl it all started with the stock market crash of 1929, it really damaged the big industrial companies and everyone lost their investments in the stocks. It was United States greatest economic crises and millions of people suffered, seniors lost their life savings when the banks collapses, the schools shut down and children went uneducated and unemployment was great.

During this time the depression affected male wage earners more severely than women workers. Industries like steel, rubber, and chemicals, which were dominated by white male workers was shut down or slowed to a crawl. This left the male workers out of their jobs and it was a lot harder for men to find work in factories during the depression than women. Women's roles were mostly as homemaker and in the workplace remained traditional. The light industries like manufacturing, service and domestic jobs where most female workers were employed and were affected less then the major companies. Women also had more wage-earning opportunities in non-industrial work such as teaching, nursing, domestic service, and office work than the men did. Traditionally with these different type jobs were not for men and the men was above taking a job that was deemed a woman's job in society.

Many ladies had to go to work for the very first time instead of staying at home like they were taught to do. They were forced to find jobs, because their husbands had been laid off or suffered from wage cuts. This was especially the case for older, married women who had left the labor force when they had children. Wages for working women was only $5 per week. Although it was easier for women to find work, than for men, there was still high unemployment among women in 1931, by 20% and by 1933, 50% of these ladies who was unemployed were solely responsible for supporting their families. In 1930 about eleven million women were employed and by 1940, thirteen million women were employed.

Society was very critical of women working during the depression for two main reasons. The first reason was that they thought women were taking men's jobs. The second reason was they felt that women workers were abandoning their families in a time of extreme need. Women workers also faced heavy discrimination and social criticism during the depression. Women who had jobs were often pressured to give up their jobs for family men. Some even blamed women for the depression itself. They were claiming that if women would give up their jobs, unemployment would be nearly eliminated. When women could find jobs they tended to be low level, low paying jobs, nearly all management roles were filled by men. When women could find jobs they tended to be low level, low paying jobs and nearly all management roles were filled by men. Census reports at the time show that three in ten working women were in domestic or personal service roles, such as cooks and maids. Of those women working outside personal service fully three quarters were school teachers or nurses. There was no protection at the time for women in the workplace, meaning they could be fired simply for being a woman without unemployment or severance. Working women also had no guarantee of equal wages or treatment.

Only about 15% of the workers hired by the Works Progress Administration (WPA) were women, and very few of them were African American women. Their work was considered unskilled, and women were paid less than men. In the late 1930s, women with children were fired in mass numbers from WPA jobs because they were supposed to be able to collect money for having child dependents, but those payments were very difficult to get, and many women were left without any incomes.

The media was totally against working mothers. They refused to recognize that the large numbers of married women who entered the labor force did so out of the necessity in an effort to save their families from starvation and homelessness. The employers thought that they could treat their employees any way that they wanted. They did not care bout the working conditions. But they did not take in mind that the women of that time were fearless because they had nothing to loose they were living at the bottom of all of the classes and there was nowhere to go but up.

The 1930s were years of employees fighting to upgrade their work environment which was really the lowest class of people fighting for their basic rights. It was a class struggle and there were great advances in the work place that was made for the working class. No decade before or since has witnessed such a growth of labor's influence and strength in the U.S. From the very beginning, women were deeply involved in these struggles of organizing the people. It started when the National Unemployed Councils brought working-class men and women together with chapters in many of the major of cities and towns who successfully fought evictions and utility shutoffs which were due to the lack of work.

Unemployment was a lot worse among African-American women because they lost their positions as domestic servants to white women who entered the market during the Depression. In urban areas, they were forced to convene on city corners called "slave markets," they were hoping to be hired for very low-paid day labor as you see the Mexicans do today. After the end of slavery black women fought for their rights in the Black Women's Suffrage Movement. Women gained the right to vote in 1920. The Jim Crow racial segregation and disenfranchisement which was enforced by extreme violence across the nation African-Americans were systematically denied the right to vote during this time and many resisted this oppression. For as long as the African woman has been in the United States they have fought oppression and they organized themselves and others to fight for freedom just as they did during the slave days.

Miss Johnston was interrupted by some costumers coming in and she had to go clean a table and make her rounds with the coffee pot. As she left she said, "I will be back to tell you about how it was organizing and fighting for your rights that had made it easy for you have what you have now and you take it so light heartily today".

CHAPTER # 2

Living the Real Life as an Adult

I ASKED SUE, "Where was I?" Sue replied, "You got picked up by a woman named Miss. Linda." Oh, ya Miss Linda was a good hearted woman who worked hard for what she got. So Miss Linda decided to offer me a job. As we where pulling in to town Linda asked me if I wanted to stay on until I made enough money to move on. With me hearing that I just lit up and said, "Yes mam, it is a blessing that you can help me out like this and I will help you with what ever you need done."

As we arrived at Miss Linda's Bed and Breakfast, I was surprised to see that Miss Linda also owned a Gas Station with a garage to do work on cars. Miss Linda's house was a big one with five bedrooms upstairs. She had the basement fixed up with 3 bedrooms and a full bathroom. This is where she let the hired hands stay. Miss Linda had three men working at the gas Station, a mechanic and two helpers who pumped gas and serviced the cars. She also had a lady help around the house with cooking and cleaning. I could see that Miss Linda really did not need my help. She must have felt sorry for me and wanted to help me out.

Only one of the men who worked at the gas station lived down stairs. The other two lived with their families in town and the housekeeper lived down stairs as well. So Miss Linda moved me in to the third bedroom. Miss Linda had her bedroom up stairs with the renters. She was doing very good business and always kept two or three rooms rented to somebody. She took our room and board out of our weekly pay. She was a real fair lady with all of us.

The next morning I was awakened with a knock on my door. It was the house keeper. Miss Linda had sent her down to tell me it was time to eat. By the time I got up stairs the other two employees were finishing up their breakfast. Miss Linda was serving us and introduced me to Mary, the house keeper and to Bob the gas station attendant. They seemed like nice people. As they went to work Miss Linda served me and her self. It was a good breakfast with juice, eggs and toast.

Miss Linda said to me, "I am running a business and you must dress to please the customers. That meant while I am working I must have no dresses or skirts on that show my legs and I must have my buttons, buttoned all of the way to the top and always wear an apron. She did not care how hot it got out side, this was the dress code. I said to my self, "God this is just like living at home." Then I realized that in my situation I must take the bitter with the sweet. I have a good deal going on here and I need it in order to survive.

Miss Linda continued with," you will be helping Mary with her chores and when you two get things caught up then you can go see Bob at the station and clean the area and Bob will teach you how to run the cash register."

We finished eating and as I was leaving Miss Linda said, "If you want to be on your own as a grown up there are still rules to follow. The more you want in life, the more a person will have to learn and follow the dress codes, proper social manners and what ever is expected by the upper class. Speaking properly is another thing you need to be accepted by the people that have the ability to give you the opportunities to better your life. Now it is time to start earning your money, go see Mary."

Mary soon realized that I had to be taught everything. She even had to give me some dresses to wear to meet Miss Linda's dress code. I really did not realize how easy I had it at home. I learned how to iron clothes today. Mary said, that she will teach me how to cook and even how to wash clothes. At home I just had to clean my room once a week or take out the garbage every other day and that was about it. Here it is cleaning rooms every day and taking out the garbage every day. God, I do not believe it, I am missing home already.

Lunch time came and it was about time. All of this work had given me a good appetite. When we got to the table to eat Bob was already there. Miss Linda had a nice lunch already for us and it was good. Bob and I keep eyeing each other and smiling. I know Miss Linda and Mary noticed it as well. It did not look like Miss Linda liked what she was seeing. Miss Linda was a strait forward woman. After we finished lunch she told all three of us, "that there will be no hanky panky going on in this house. We are to stay out of each others rooms at all times and if we are caught then it might cost us our jobs. We are all adults here and we are going to give the respect that is due to each other." She looked us all in the eye and got us to say, "Yes or O.K."

After lunch Miss Linda sent Mary and me out to do yard work till it was time to make dinner. I felt that Miss Linda did not want Bob and I to get to know each other. Mary and I went outside and started pulling weeds and raking the leaves in the yard. I could see Bob attending to cars from the front yard. Again we had eye to eye contact and we both were smiling about it again. I was looking forward to seeing him at dinner time. Mary caught us looking at each other and said, "The more you think about your job, the faster time will go by and the sooner you can see the young man. Try it and you will see that I am right." So I took her advice and kept my mind on the work I was doing.

The next thing I knew, Mary was telling me "come let's make dinner." Mary and I were a good team and with my help she said, it makes her day a lot easier. We made dinner and served the guests. I was looking forward to eating with Bob but he never came in to eat. We had to wait until after the guests ate, so Mary said, "There is no reason to be standing around and watching them eat. Come help me clean the kitchen." After washing the pot and pans, Mary handed me a plate of food and said, "Take this to Bob and do not forget to give him something to drink." I got so happy that Mary had to stop me from leaving with out a napkin and the silverware.

As I was walking over to the gas station, I could see Jim the mechanic closing the shop and Bob was pumping gas in a car. I took the food in to the station and introduced my self to Jim.

Jim said, "All Bob talked about all day was the new girl and asked me all kinds of questions, like who is she? Where did she come from? Do you think she has a boyfriend? And so on and so on." Bob was getting on Jims nerves. Well, I did not tell Jim but I had the same questions about Bob. Jim started heading home and Bob had a break to eat. We started talking about every thing. Bob and I kept eyeing each other and smiling and we could not stop. Miss Linda came in to count the money. Right off the bat she told me to, "Go back to the house and finish with Mary." I know Miss Linda was watching us through the window as she was walking up to the gas station. She noticed us looking and smiling as well. As I was leaving she said to us "You two little love birds will have plenty of time to get to know each other in the weeks to come, now scat Betty." She was right. After finishing the day with Mary, Bob and I did have some time to get to know each other at the end of each day.

Days turned in to weeks and weeks turned in to months. Going in to the third month Bob asked me, "to be his girlfriend" and of course I said, "Yes." Bob and I had a good relationship together. We spent every moment we could together. We even broke the house rule about not entering each others room. One thing leads to the next and before I knew it we were having sex. Mary caught Bob coming out of my room one morning. Mary told me and Bob, "That she will not have babies raising babies around her and we have one more chance. You two stay out of each others room."

Bob worked it out for him and I to have the same days off so we could do things together. One time he took me to downtown to have dinner and see a movie. It was the first time some one treated me to an evening like that. The next morning I found my self running to the bathroom and throwing up I thought that it might be the food we ate the night before but when I talked to Bob about it he was not sick. The sickness lasted for weeks but it was just in the morning and I was beginning to get worried so I asked Mary. Mary said, "Oh my god, you have morning sickness" and I thought she was talking about something like the cold or flu that everyone gets. She said, "Stupid, you are pregnant" and when she said that, my whole world stopped.

When I told Bob that I was pregnant he was surprised too. After talking to him I found out that he did not want to accept the reasonability for raising a child. He wanted me to get rid of it. Bob said, "We are two teenagers who can barely feed our selves and now we must feed a baby." When I found that out I knew that I was I big trouble. What was Miss Linda going to say or even worse what is she going to do? And how was I going to raise a child on my own if Bob does not help?

Mary kept the news from Miss Linda for me, but she wanted me to tell Miss Linda. I kept putting it off for one reason or another and after several weeks Mary was getting tired of me not acting as an adult. So Mary told me that she would not keep my secret any longer. I knew that it was only a matter of time before Miss Linda could see that I was pregnant.

Bob was my first love so I was playing the part of an immature self centered young teenager, who was drunk with love. I would do any and every thing to please my man as I was taught from watching my parents. I knew that my job in a relationship was to follow the leader and do what I was told to do. I was just the opposite of Miss Linda. I knew that Miss Linda's rules were for my own good but I let my emotions get in the way. I am not supposed to let my emotions lead me in my life and in doing so it means that I have very little will power over my emotions. Adults are supposed to have control of their emotions or at least have control to a major degree. That is what growing up is all about, learning how to control your emotions in your childhood and teens.

These puppy love emotions lead all young people in to trouble. Young people must realize that the teen years is mainly about learning how to control your emotions while you are under the shelter of the family so you will have control before you get out there in the real adult world. Every body needs this control because with out it they will find themselves in trouble time after time until they do learn. A lot of people do not accomplish this until they are in their late teens or early twenties. That is if they have family support during that time. Those with out the family support will not accomplish controlling their emotions until they are well in their twenties or thirties. For those hard headed people, who are self centered, they may never accomplish this control and their lives will always have major trouble in it until the end. Any way, back to the story.

I was not Bob's first love. He knew it was my first love and he felt it was his job, as far as being a man in those days, to take full advantage of the situation. So, Bob laid down the law and said, "It is my way or no way" and with me being so rum dumb in love, I said, "Okay." Bob was not following his emotions, he was following his wisdom. He knew that he would have to sacrifice everything, his time, his money, his wants and his needs in order to raise a family. This is what every parent must do to raise their children to be well rounded mentally, socially, spiritually and physically.

I did not want to abort the baby. I was hoping that Bob would change his mind once he saw the baby even though Bob told me of the hardships that lie ahead if we kept the baby. To me, I understood, but I really did not realize or picture the future as an adult. I should have thought about not having sex, as an adult and not follow my emotion of love, as a teenager. If I would have thought like an adult, I would not be pregnant now.

One day I was working the cash register at the gas station because things were slow in the house. It was a time was I was starting to show. Like clock-work Miss Linda came in to count the money. This time Miss Linda decided that it is time to speak up and tell it as she sees it. Miss Linda asked me if I thought that she was blind and dumb. Since you want to play games, lie, break the rules and hide things from me I will have to let you go. I can not have an employee live here with a child crying in the middle of the night disturbing the guests and them doing half of their job because they have to tend to their child. Bob walked in and Miss Linda asked "do you two know that you're way too young to have this child? I have to let the both of you go. You can stay the night and in the morning after breakfast you can go. I will have your money for this week at that time."

I had to stop my story and tell Sue, "It is very important that you really under stand that our life is affected by the world around us, with the rules and beliefs of society, our family, our friends, our work place and our religion. Each one of these influences and creates cycles which intertwine with one another. We must live our lives within these cycles to make things work. It is very important for you to learn as much as possible through education in your teenage days. You do not want to waste your time reeducating your self at a later age. You need to have a good understanding of the rules and expectation of employers, our government, organizations and society. This is why you must break the negative cycles that are in your daily life. So your children understand why they need to learn about listening, following orders, controlling their emotions, social manors, etc., etc., etc. while living at home.

Consciousness of your future will show you where you do want to be 50 years down the road. You must start planning ahead as a teenager. You must start thinking what you might want to do or what type of job you would really want. Then you need to see what is really required for that kind of job. You need to know who you are how you got here so you can change any negative cycles that are in your life that might interfere with your goals. Most likely these negative cycles were pasted down to you from your parents. By being honest with your self about your family history you can change where you are going in order to be a person who knows where they will be in the future and knows the future of their grandchildren. We need to change this cycle of fear of the churches, government and our social media. Any body can do this and really believe in their selves as individuals. Remember self-reliance is self-respect."

Half way through breakfast it started raining real hard. So, I suggested to Sue to, "Stay and chat with me until the rain lets up". Sue said, "Okay." because she had no where to go anyway and the last thing she needed was to get all cold and wet.

Then Miss Johnston came by to refresh our coffees and of course get to get back in to our conversation. With out missing a lick she started back in on woman's rights. "You know that when the working lady was standing up for their rights they was labeled as being under the influence of the growth of the militant, communist-led Housewives by the white males across the land. They were seen as ladies breaking up families and taking away the jobs meant for men."

In 1933 President Roosevelt took office and greatly changed women's experience in the work force and in labor unions by starting the New Deal Program and that was only because his wife hounded him to do the right thing. The New Deal in many ways greatly aided women workers during the Great Depression which included, the National Recovery Administration (NRA) with its industrial codes, the Wagner Act, which placed the federal government behind labor unions and collective bargaining, the Works Progress Administration (WPA), which created government jobs for unemployed men and women, the Fair Labor Standards Act set minimum wage and maximum hours standards for industrial workers and the Social Security Program, which initiated retirement pensions, disability insurance, and payments for single mothers with dependent children, widows, women with disabled husbands, and single mothers began to receive monthly Social Security payments.

The New Deal also had a positive effect on women's involvement in organized labor. The Congress of Industrial Organizations (CIO) was founded during the New Deal period and organized entire industries rather than single crafts, meaning that unskilled women in the auto, rubber, metal, leather, and glass industries were included in CIO unions alongside male workers. The United Auto Workers and the United Electrical Workers included women in especially large numbers. The NRA and the Wagner Act's backing of organized labor both strengthened traditionally female labor unions and helped women get more involved in male-dominated unions. The International Ladies Garment Worker's Union experienced a second wave of successful organizing to regulate hours, improve wages, slow down production rates, and outlaw mandatory overtime for women working in the needle trades.

Out of no were a customer at the counter yells out, "Oh come on Missy I need another cup of coffee." Miss Johnston turns to him and says, "You have all ready had four cups of coffee and you know that only the second cup is free. You need to slow down before you start pissen like a race horse."

She then turned back to us to finish what she wanted to say, "In 1934, the American Federation of Labor (AFL) decided to expand its roster of women workers and even chartered the New York Domestic Workers' Union. Black and white male and female sharecroppers organized the Southern Tenant Farmers Union. Women unionists were major organizers which raised wages and convinced the government to establish an investigatory commission to study the plight of southern sharecroppers. In 1937, the CIO gave charters to three white-collar, all-female unions, including the United Office and Professional Workers of America (UOPWA), which initiated successful wage and hour strikes in mailing firms and publishing houses nationwide. By 1940, almost eight hundred, thousand American women workers were unionized which was triple the number before the New Deal programs started.

The New Deal started programs that improved women's collective bargaining efforts, encouraged more women from more industries to unionize, and encouraged traditionally male national unions to include women and improved women's experiences in industry in many ways, its programs were plagued with sexism and racism and therefore preserved prejudices against women, especially African American women, in the work force. Roosevelt started the well needed health regulations for the meat industries to help stop dieses for spreading ramped across the nation. He got a heavy negative response from all of the republicans in congress because of the pressure the industrialist. They had to spend extra money to abide by the new laws. With President Roosevelt being a republican this New Deal coast him his 2nd term in office." Just because he wanted to do what was right for the people. It just goes to show that the republicans back then is still the same way to day. It is all about making the buck for business no matter who gets heart.

The man at the counter calls out again. Miss Johnston replies with, " Hold on to your horses, as many cups that you had the police is going to stop you from walking to fast down the street because you are beginning to act like a speed junky" as she is walking to refill his cup. She kept talking and serving the coffee, "There were years of fierce class struggle and, women were deeply involved in these struggles which led to great advances for the working class. No decade before or since has witnessed such an expansion of labor's influence and strength in the U.S. The Unemployed Councils brought working-class men and women together. The National Unemployed Council, with chapters in scores of cities and towns and all but four states, successfully fought evictions and utility shutoffs.

The Detroit black women's Housewives League was founded in 1930 by Fannie Peck, and in 5 years, the League had over 10,000 members. The Detroit Housewives League took on the meatpacking industry itself. In 1935, the group burned a huge packing house in protest of high prices, and they joined thousands of Chicago housewives in a march that shut down that entire meat industry within Chicago. Nationwide, these Leagues created 75,000 jobs for Black Americans, overcoming racial discrimination.

By September 1937, the two-year old Committee on Industrial Organization (CIO later changed to Congress of Industrial Organizations), had more then 3.7 million members. Among them were half a million

Black workers and hundreds of thousands of Asians and Latinos. There were immigrants from all over some 400,000 from Poland alone.

In 1937 the Flint sit down strike was the first sit down strike of a mainly female workforce. They were the cigar workers of Detroit with 4,000 women mostly Polish. They went on strike for better hours, better pay, better ventilation, and better toilet facilities. After a long fight with people going to jail and the hospital or both, they got their union contract. These ladies inspired other women to strike in the Detroit area at Ferry-Mors Seed, Woolworth who had forty stores in the area, as well as, Hotel and Restaurant workers. They too received raises in pay, seniority rights, shorter hours, uniforms provided by the company and future hiring through the unions. The strikes with the department store workers spread across the nation to office workers and factory workers and they won union contracts.

The organizer for the Workers Alliance was Miss. Emma Tenayuca and in 1938 lead the Pecan Sheller's strike against 147 shops with over 11,000 workers who worked seventy hours a week for thirty cents a day, they had no civil rights and were starving. They won their fight and set standards across the nation for field workers.

Well ladies, I really do have to go back to work, but I will be back and to tell you the truth about it what I am telling you is just the icing on the cake. The true amount of sacrifices that was made is far from being known. I am talking about mental, physical, social, financial and spiritual sacrifices and the affect it had on millions of people in every way thinkable. They did it for them self's and for the generations to come.

The vast majority of women workers in the depression did not enjoy wage increases or 40-hour weeks but thanks to the unions these issues were being addressed. At the end of World War II, more women were working and organized than ever before. As their experiences during the Great Depression, the New Deal era show and World War II women in the 1930s and 1940s still faced the same sexism and racism that had plagued American women. During this time women workers enjoyed a higher status within organized labor industry but their wage and hour codes did not apply to the non-industrial work, such as agriculture, domestic service, nursing, and clerical work, where most women were employed.

With that being said, Miss Johnston went back to work and Betty went back to her life story with Sue.

CHAPTER # 3

Making Babies

WE FOUND A little one bedroom apartment. Bob found a job right away but I had a hard time finding a job because nobody wanted to hire a pregnant teenage girl. I gave all of my money that I was saving from working at Miss Linda's to help move in to an apartment. Bob's friends from the gas station helped us with some furniture and Mary came by with Miss Linda with enough food to stock our cupboards. They all were a true blessing.

Due to the depression, businesses all over started slowly laying off their workers and closing their doors. Bob had to take a cut in his wages in order to keep his new job as a gas station attendant. I started baby sitting and washing and ironing the neighbor's clothes to help make ends meet but we were still slowly falling behind. I finally had the baby and she was the sweetest little thing that I had ever seen. Thank God, I did not have a hard time getting Bob to help me with the baby. He did what ever he could to help but I could see in his face that it was slowly driving him crazy. He soon got laid off from his job and he decided to go find work somewhere even if it meant leaving the state. Bob was irritated because he had a family and no job. He searched high and low for a job around the town and county. Finally Bob made his move, leaving me by myself to contend with the baby. He told me that he would send money when he could and he did just that. It just was not enough. We fell behind on the rent, the lights were cut off and the only food was from the local church.

I had put off the landlord as long as I could and it was time to move but to where?

I was doing volunteer work at the church for several months before I lost my apartment and I found a nice lady there who I asked to take care of my baby because I had no home for her and I could not feed or care for her. The lady said, "Yes". I told the lady, "As soon as I get on my feet I will come get the baby." It hurt me deeply to leave my baby but I figured the baby was better off with the lady who had a family and a good man who had been working for the city for a long time.

I finally got a letter from Bob saying that he was in California but he did not send money. He did not say for me to come be with him and I felt I had to do something. I kept in contact with Bob and with him being my first love and the father of my child it made everything a lot harder. I could not put him out of my mind. I had come to the conclusion that I was going to try to get to Bob and then we could save enough money to get our baby back. To make a long story short when I got back with Bob he thought that the baby was better off with the family that was taking care of her. He wanted us to go on living our life with out the baby.

I found a job in Long Beach. I got a job cooking and Bob got a job selling homes as a real state agent. It started out alright until I had accidently got pregnant again. Bob tried to help out as much as he could but Bob and I had two different ways of raising a child. As the years started going by I had another accident and got pregnant again. It was still a hard life as it was and now as all working parents know just having some body watch the baby, getting baby food, dipper service alone took almost all of the money I made. We tried hard to make things work. As time went on, Miss Linda's two love birds found them selves drifting further apart.

This time I left Bob. It did not take long for me to meet another man. I kept my job as a cook and met a co-worker named Mark and we started dating. I took it slow because of the baby. As time went on everything was looking good. So, Mark and I got a nice little house and we started making more babies. We made four kids in the ten years we were together. I guess that the kids were getting to be too much for Mark but we loved our sex and due to that we kept having babies. I know this is what drove Mark to drink. With a couple of years of drinking that slowly got worse, we both knew that it was time to go our separate ways.

One day I was sitting on the porch and the living room window was wide open and Mark had a friend over. They were on the couch drinking and I heard Marks friend telling him that his sister in law was put in an insane asylum because his brother was just too tired of her. The husband took the wife to the doctor complaining about her being too emotional and the wife was just trying to tell the doctor that it was due to her husband drinking and cheating on her. The doctor told her to calm down and quit raising her voice. The doctor prescribed some medicine for the woman's emotions and the woman refused to take it repeating that the husband was the problem. The doctor insisted and the woman refused again. Than the doctor committed the woman for psychiatric therapy and the more the woman fought back the more the doctors pumped her with drugs. The woman went through shock therapy and a couple of months later the doctors did a frontal lobotomy on her and she was turned in to a vegetable. It was common practice for husbands, police or social services to commit women in the early and well into the mid1900s. Marks friend then said maybe you should have Betty committed.

After hearing that I studied on the subject and found that in the 1940s a board of psychiatrist got together to make money off the government for research with the mentally ill. The book called (DSM) Diagnostic and Statistical Manual of Mental Disorders and was used as guide lines on all emotional problems for the psychiatrist across the nation and abroad. Every ten years or so the board would add new theories put out in an updated book. The government started out with one million dollars per year to fund the research and now in the late 1980s they get 4 billion a year from the government. The pharmaceutical industry was behind it all because then they could have their new drug tried out on these people with the government paying the bill.

It is big business with the psychiatric doctors and research corporations. The doctors and companies are making their money off of these ADD or ADHD kids. The drugs that they give the kids are as strong and addictive as heroin. The diagnose of ADD and ADHD keeps changing because the board members of the (DSM) Diagnostic and Statistical Manual of Mental Disorders, which is the holy bible of mental disorders can not agree on what is the cause of any one symptom.

Any body, who is sane, can be ruled as having ADD or ADHD if they are examined when they are very emotional over a personal problem. The school examination is only five minutes long and the nurses are only looking at how the kid is acting at that time. She is not looking at why the child is acting this way. Once your kid is admitted it is really hard to take the kid out of the program even if the kid is not showing any illness. The parents lose their rights in this matter.

It is a fact that most of the kids with ADD or ADHD are fatherless. Most of children disorders come from single parent families. A lot of mothers can not work for a living, then go home and care properly for their kids. The kids are staying up late; drinking a lot of sodas and the mother is too tired to stick to their rules of discipline in order to raise the kid's right. The people need to wake up and see that most of thee kids do not have emotional problems due to mental disorder but to lack of discipline, family structure, family values, money problems and lack of a father.

Thank god there is an organization called CCHR International who is like the watch dog of these crooks. If you want to help the people you should go to school to be an Education Lawyer to help these families with the school programs and the big business with the psychiatric doctors and drug research corporations. Hell a couple of my kids would have been labeled as having ADD or ADHD and they turned out to be good people. Here I am getting deep in to one subject and not getting on with the story. I am sorry but the government needs to stop funding these people.

Mark got a lot worse with his drinking so we had to go our separate ways. Mark was nice enough to give us the car. Both fathers saw there kids and helped out a lot with the bills and food when ever they could. As time went on the children saw less and less of their fathers. I remember Mark leaving, it was after having a big argument and he didn't even take the time to say goodbye to the kids. Mark was walking away from home for good. I remember his son ran out to the main street and for as little as he was, it was a long run that must have seemed like forever to him. In reality it was probably two or three blocks. The boy was crying the whole way going "dad, dad give me a hug" he finally caught up with his father. It was a big strong passionate hug. They did not say anything but they knew it would be a long time before they see each other again and then Mark sent him back home. You could see in the boys face that he was glad to have that hug before his dad left.

As the years started to go by I worked as a cook. The doctor told me that I had to stop standing for long periods of time due to my varicose veins. Since I could not work and the men left me with all of these children I was forced get on welfare. This only covered the rent and food that only lasted a few weeks. So I had to start writing checks in order to make ends meet. The money that was coming in from their fathers was helping but it was not enough. Now we were really struggling to get help that would get us get enough food to last through the month.

The law started to catch up with me for writing bad checks so we had to move on or have our family broken up. If I had gotten caught the government would have put the kids in different homes. I sweet talked men to create a bill and moved on before it was time to pay up and begged at the churches to keep my kids fed, clothed and a roof over their head.

Miss. Johnson stopped one more time to get in on the conversation. She started with the woman's rights movement despite society's discrimination against women; they played a big part in during WWII. For example, my grand mother and mother was deep in to women's rights and if it was not for ladies like them we would not have the rights that we have today. In 1941 because of a coalition of African American men and women, President Roosevelt created the Fair Employment Practices Commission, which made it illegal for a government sub-contracted industry to discriminate against blacks. The Commission enabled African-American women to get the higher-paid jobs in industry that they had been excluded from for so long. The attack at Pearl Harbor in 1941, deepen and extended the women's experiences in industry because the United States needed a great military force that would take men out of the work force. The men were drafted to go to war and the factories were gearing up to make war materials. That left mostly ladies to work on the production lines. They took over the jobs that was dominated by men in the past. They proved that they are able to do the same work as men and just as good. As the demand for workers grew the government changed their view from not letting house wife's work to being more then happy to have them working. The female work force grew 50%; six million women joined the work force.

They began to recruit women into heavy industries, chemicals, rubber, and petroleum to take the place of the men in both military and civilian jobs. All around the country, women stepped into government jobs vacated by men. More than a million women, many of them young and single, came to Washington D.C. As more men were deployed overseas for jobs like clerical positions. Women served as radio operators, air traffic controllers, planners, and educators who provided training. They worked in crucial positions in intelligence gathering, analysis, cryptography, research and laboratory testing that led to scientific advances and inventions that saved lives.

In 1943 there still were dangerous working conditions in the work place, less pay for the same work as men and sexual harassment. Society and industry had always seen the female workers as temporary help until the soldiers came back. The women's roll in the war work force had brought them closer to being equal.

The United Auto Workers had established a Women's Bureau in its War Policy Division in 1944 and it addressed equal pay between male and female workers. The organized labor industry expanded to the United Packinghouse Workers of America, the United Electrical Workers, American Federation of Teachers, the CIO and they expanded their agendas to include lobbying for national health insurance, free daycare for working mothers, and maternity leave.

By the end of World War II, more women were working and more women were organized than ever before. There are a lot of society's leaders today that feel the woman's place should be at home and the white man will always be supreme in this land of mixed races and women. The media is controlled by the major industries and the government who wants to keep the past alive with the white man at the top of the social ladder. That is why working women were rarely seen on TV or in the movies in the 1900's. In the 1950's it was common for companies to have a written policy that stated ladies will not get paid as much as men. On the average at the time women got 60% of what men got and today the percentage is higher but still not equal to the men. With the pressure from families, society and companies the effort of the woman's movement died down until the 1960's. In 1963 the Equal Pay Act was passed but to this day in a lot of work places it is still not enforced. In the 1960's 3.5% was lawyers and only 2% of business executives was ladies. In 2004 30% of lawyers were women and 73% of the white collar jobs were women. In the 1980's women earned more bachelor and master's degrees then men. In 2004 58% of bachelor and master's degrees was given to women and 44% of all doctoral degrees went to ladies too.

CHAPTER # 4

Hard Times Raising Children

WE MOVED TO Watts Ville, CA in the early 1950s. It was a surprise to all of us because two thirds of the land around us was farms and we were actually city or big town folk. Out there at that time it was a time of change because the farmers started selling their farms and they started building low income homes for the blacks to keep them from moving in to the city. I come to find out that a black family could not live any were they wanted to back in those days because they had exceptions in their housing contracts and zoning laws that stopped people of color from moving in to the city and hate groups of the day ran free to do as they pleased to any one walking those streets.

We lived a block from the main part of town, which was really some business's that lined the highway for several blocks that ran from Los Angeles to Long Beach. It's nothing like what you'd expect hearing of the history of a place like Watts. This was downtown for Watts Ville.

I had to find a place to live but the money I was getting from welfare did not allow me to move into a nice middle class neighborhood. I finally found a little house were we could afford the rent. The owner of the house was a black man named George and every one called him junk man George. They called him that because he went around the streets collecting bottles and metals to recycle. He also sold fruit from his pickup which helped him pay the bills because his retirement check from the railroad was not enough for him.

He had two houses on his property. He lived in the house in the front and we lived in the house in the back. Both houses had two small bedrooms. It was tight for me and my kids but it was a roof over our heads. The children never had enough food so George would help out by giving us fruit when he could. I had to get most of our food and clothes from the local churches. I had to depend on my oldest son who was in his mid teens. I was thankful to have him to watch the others as I looked for work, food and clothing for the kids. One good thing about it was that as the years went by I got more and more help from the older children.

Thanks to Social Security Insurance, I had medical for the kids, a monthly check to pay the rent and to help out with the utilities and enough food to last two or three weeks each month. The last week of the month usually meant eating the same thing for breakfast, lunch and dinner. One thing that was in my favor was that the children understood the situation that we were in. The down side to being on welfare is that they give you barely enough to live on. That is if you live in an old part of town where the rent is very cheap.

My oldest son Paul and my daughter Julie was in their teens at this time. They played dictionary games pronouncing words and she made the boys read. This really was a blessing because it helped the kids in their education. I remember I would have everyone take a nap and I would come in and mention that whoever is asleep could have ice cream. I know that if they were awake they couldn't say anything about it because if they did then I knew that they were not asleep. It was my way of making them take a nap. When I look back you could say that I did bribe them to do the right thing.

I got a new boy friend. He got me pregnant twice and both of my black sons was born in our house. Thank god for mid-wife's. During the birth of them I had to send my children to a friend named Debbie. She was a neighbor who lived in a nice farm house and I remember my children always complaining about her. She kept the kids around her all the time and she would have the kids help out with the chores.

They were always working. She always tried to give them fresh milk and nothing is worse than worm fresh milk out of a cow when you are a kid. She would always have a pitcher of warm milk for them. It was really terrible for the kids because they were city kids used to cold store bought milk.

I feel sorry about the way the blacks were treated in those days. There I go getting carried away and off the subject. Sue looked out side at the rain and said, "No it is okay, I would like to hear the rest of it." So they had a refill of coffee and Betty went back to her life story.

It was a black community and over all they treated us fairly. I had met some black women who had kids like me and we all had no man to help us raise the children right. We would sit at each others houses once a week just to relax and catch up with the gossip over a beer. After a while I came to realize that the white society was holding back the black race any way that they could. I have seen wrong doings and heard the statements from people who had first hand knowledge of the harassment and racism that held a hard working black parent back from raising their family as one should. Due to the police and white aggression through desegregation which was keep the black people subconsciously feeling the sense of elimination from the normal American civilization or in other words blacks started feeling like the lowest class of all the citizens. This is still being planned and carried out by the elite organizations nationally and locally, today.

From 1950-1966 the police was run like a military unit across the nation. It was their job to help the politicians and business by giving all colored people a record to hinder their employment and success in life by keeping the black man down if not separated from his family. It was a time that was devastating for many black families that lived in poverty. Many black men could not support their families because the jobs where taken by the higher ranking classes of people in society. For example the whites always got the best jobs, then the white woman then the white immigrants and all that was left was service jobs and black ladies was loosing their jobs to white ladies who needed to feed their families. Many black women become the head family provider. That left the black men to scratch out a income or should I say to learn how to hustle for the money. Now in these days with generation after generation of single parent families the men finding that their father or grand father hustled for money, they automatically follow their ways. This is a cycle that needs to stop. A person needs education and jobs in order to make this change.

The police knew that if you are not a working person, you will have to do any thing to feed their children and in many cases this meant breaking the law. The police were treating black people (men and women) as if they were truly at war. Keep in mind that the US still had segregation until the late1960s meaning you could not eat, walk, talk, sit and drink anywhere you wanted to, like you can today. If you were seen in a white neighborhood the police would stop you and if you showed any self pride or did not show the police that you had great fear of them they felt that it was their job to put the fear into anybody who did not treat them as gods. Some examples are; if you were black you could not go to downtown unless you had a working pass, or for the simplest violation of five miles over the speed limit, riding around with more than three people in the car. Asking questions about your rights was taken as aggression and standing up for your rights meant jail time or getting beat up at the very least. Whatever they could find to fine you with, they did. Records on individuals were adding up fast and that in the eyes of the law this means habitual criminals. Even though there was robbery and murder, most of the crimes were very petty but they added up. This gave the employers an excuse not to hire you. It also made sure that you will never get a good paying job because of your criminal record which stays with you for life. This is true economical and mental slavery in the true educational sense.

Another example is the racial lines in society like the term we all hear, wrong side of the tracks or the avenue called "Alameda" in Los Angeles, California. On one side of the avenue or the tracks was black and the other side of the line were whites only. Any one in almost any city could find this racial line. In the evenings if you got caught on the wrong side of the line the police treated you even worse. In that time period it was no secret, everyone knew the rules.

Through generations of suppression this feeling is imbedded into your subconscious state of mind. People treated like this are culturally disoriented with no sense of identity of who they really are. Most of the jobs were the lowest paying jobs and the most demeaning jobs, like most of all of the jobs given to blacks through out history. It is a fact that after years of this, a person or a race would get a deep sense of self-hatred because you see yourself having almost no value in the community or in society. Now, in these days with generation after generation of single parent families this feeling lay's in the subconscious part of the mind creating an unknown feeling deep down. For example: the kids of the black neighborhoods in the 1950s and 1960s did not have organizations like the Boy Scouts, Cub Scouts and the YMCA to join and did not have a sense of direction or mentoring in the way a young man should live his life like the kids in the white neighborhoods did. So, the teenagers started their own group organization called gangs to have something to do in their spare time. Even in the 1990's you could find 125 high schools in California that do not have AP classes to pass the test to go to college. You will find these high schools in colored neighborhoods, not in the white neighborhoods. That is in reference just to one state and there are many states that are worse.

African-American women have had a long tradition of civil and human rights activism. Black women's militant activism and leadership during this oppression helped create the Civil Rights movement of the 20th century. The organizational skills and grassroots activism of women such as Septima Clark, Rosa Parks, Ella Baker Eleanor Norton, Angela Davis, Fannie Hammer and Alice Walker pushed the movement forward to many successes and inspired a new generation of activists.

That tradition of taking charge lives on today in the experiences and examples of women with having to deal with their families. In the 1950s and 1960s the black American family structure was being dominated and controlled by outspoken women. Despite the risk of great personal loss the role of motherhood that black women of this time period were expected to fulfill the image of the a strong woman, like the image of Big Momma. The black mother was someone who had to be a traditional good mother: nurturing and caring towards her children, but at the same time she was considered unfeminine, strong willed and domineering.

Miss Johnston had some free time and stopped at our table to give us more coffee and to listen to our conversation. She then started in with her point of view on the sacrifices of the black race.

The black woman had to sacrifice more for their family because it was still a lot harder for black men to get a good paying job during and after WWII due to having a record on them which in turn became a reason to be denied employment of most companies and all government jobs. The black men felt they were a failure to their family, society and themselves, as the white men did during the depression, but to a much greater degree. So, the woman had to keep working even after the war was over. While the white house wife went back to their families or took the jobs of black men and ladies because the white men came home from the war and took the jobs from the white woman.

In the 1960's the reawaking of the woman rights movement for equality in the work place, home and society. The black woman was more concern with racial discrimination. It was so big of a problem that the organization (NOW) National Organization for Woman was started to address feminist and civil rights motives to cater to all women in America for the over all improvement of society.

The establishment got smarter by the studies in the past 20 years. They learned why do aliens who come here have the same health or better than elite? After being here 2 to 3 years and feeling the stress and eating the American food they start to have the same health problems as blacks who were born here. 100's of health studies show that with the accumulative affect of poor living conditions has an independent affect on health and that causes the excess release of hormones like cortisone build up, which helps plaque build up in the arteries, which is related to hypertension, which is related to heart disease and strokes. The accumulative affects is called the studies and cycles of weathering which all the doctors and organizations keep hush, hush. This is a form of brain washing via the media and organizations that is still used today.

We as individuals, races and different classes of people must work on stopping this cycle for our own families. We want our children to have the opportunity to be successful in life with whole, well rounded families and not worrying about their health. The middle and the poor class families find themselves not motivated due to self-blame, self-negativity, self-alienation, self-hatred, loss of self-confidence, which lead to hating your self because you think the whole world is like that. Once you do get your fill, who do you take it out on? Most of the times it was the helpless; young woman; children; your neighborhood is the target of the anger. The middle and the poor class families of all races must ask the self's when you are going to attack the cause of your anger, frustration and hatred? This was and still is being done through the economics of mental slavery in the true educational sense, brain washing.

The names of people's races are very important to all people because it connects them to a specific land mass, language, history, culture, philosophy and concept of God. The most affected of all the conquered races are the black people of America and Europe. All they know is their conquers culture, language, history and their concept of god. There is not a black land, Negro land, or colored land. American Japanese, German, Spanish, French, Chinese, etc., etc., etc. has names that connects them to a specific land mass, language, history, culture, philosophy and concept of God. I strongly believe that everyone should know about their own race culture and if you are from two or more races, then you should know about each one of them. The benefit to that is you will be smarter, wiser, and more open minded to all of the different concepts of all the different issues of the world.

A strong sense of self worth creates the will power to improve your self and those around you. The lower classes need to be teaching, training and showing the way to develop a strong adult relationship among married couples and teaching the teenagers the means to change the cycles of all of these negative emotional habits that keep our souls earthbound in a self-created ego prison with the bars molded out of negative thoughts or bad habits. Any limitations that we perceive are only in our minds. Change your thoughts and you change your life in the developing a positive self which could lead to running a whole family. For those who have a whole family you need to inspire those with dysfunctional families in some way by showing them what works for you and it might give them or their children some ideas on how they may achieve a whole, well rounded family too.

I had to cut in and tell the girls, "O.K. Miss Johnston you are getting way to deep, but it crossed my mind all the time, how a lot of the white people would badly treat my white children just because I had two black children. Students at their schools, the student parents, the neighbors, people walking down the street and the police most of them looked at us as white trash. They were not shy talking about you as we walked by. Now in these days, they keep it to them self's, but that does not mean that they are not thinking about it and some times they say it with their eyes.

My kids were almost the only white kids in the school and they were the only whites in their classes. I remember one of my boys would play a game and run around hitting other kids in the arm to make them chase him around the school. When he grew up he set a high school record in track which has not been broken in over twenty years. He was a natural runner. One time he ran into some other boys after school and one of them wanted to fight. One of my daughters saw what was happening and went to the aid of her brother only to embarrass him because she end up beating up the boy who wanted to fight. My son had a hard time living that down. He was upset about it for a long time.

I left Watts Ville with two new children. We had the trunk so full that the trunk lid was all of the way open and we had things packed between the rear window and the lid of the trunk. To top it off we had put our things in wooden fruit boxes which were stacked covering the whole roof of the car. All of this was tied down with rope. All of the pillows and blankets were packed around the children.

After my oldest son helped with packing the car, we all said our good byes. I felt real bad leaving him, but I knew that he was much better off with his dad. My son hoped on his bike and followed us for several blocks. You could see in his eyes that we will be very dearly missed. For the next hour all we talked about was leaving my oldest boy and how much he will be missed. The other boys did not have someone to gang them up side down and swing them around. Every once in a while when they did it in the house some body would get banged up because there just was not enough room in the house to play like that. When ever they tried to play that way in the house their sisters met them with a fist that was not to be played with.

I remember my oldest son used to drive Marks car around in the field in the back of the house when Mark was asleep. One night my son and his friend drove the car all of the way to Hollywood and they were having a great time seeing the lights and all of the people walking along the street. The next thing they knew the car stopped running and they could not start it back up right there in the middle of the street. They did not realize that there was a cop car right behind them. The boys were very lucky the police took pity on them. The policemen knew the trouble that they were already in with their parents. Mark went to get his car only to find out that the reason it stopped running was that it was out of gas. Wait until your child becomes a teenager. One thing you must remember is that the more you spoil your child the worst they will be when they become a teenager and I found this out the hard way. Although I was lucky to have all of my children grow up to be law biding, hard working and loving people who raised their families better than I did.

CHAPTER # 5

Growing Pains

IT WAS A long drive up to the Bay Area. The car was so loaded down that the body of the car was almost sitting on the tires. I could not drive over thirty miles an hour because the body of the car would rub against the tires every time we hit a bump in the road. Once we got there we could not find an apartment that would accept all of us. We stayed in the car for several days. I would leave the kids at a park to play while I looked for a house. Finally I found one but the bad thing about it is that it took all of my welfare money to pay the rent.

We moved to just outside of Hayward after Watts, it was a nice neighborhood. We got a house that was behind a little store. We got a house that was behind a little store. The children were in heaven because the house was much larger than the one in Watts Ville. The girls had a room all to themselves, the two oldest boys had their own room and the two little ones stayed with me in my room. I got a house that was set back off the street and had a big ole second back yard that had fruit trees all over it. I remember telling the kids, "If you keep eat'n that fruit your gonna get sick." They'd say, "Ya", and go out there and get sick. They were having fun in that yard because it had three foot tall grass too. They would have trails and play hide and seek. Kain was just learning how to climb trees like his older brothers and sisters. He was in a peach tree one time when he bit in to a peach and his mouth started stinging. He soon realized that he was covered with red ants. He fell out of the tree spiting, crying and slapping the ants off of him. It was funny but I also felt so sorry for him.

While we lived there I was constantly kept busy always trying to keep cloths on the kids back, food on the table and I must admit that the fruit trees really helped out in that department, keeping the kids doing good in school and a roof over their head. Times were really hard. I lost the support of the kids fathers so I had to go out to the neighborhood organizations to make up for what the welfare did not cover, and believe me it was a lot. We had a lot of bad times that out weighed the good times. That is because I never had the money to get what the kids really wanted. Year after year they would see their friends getting what they wanted from their parents for their birth days or Christmas. It takes a lot of money to raise several children.

I remember most Christmas's were disappointing to the kids because they never got what they wanted. I would make sure we all had toys and everything but they always wanted something special and it wasn't there. I would have to tell them, "Just make due with these things and one of these Christmas's you will get what you really want".

Most Christmas's it was the older kids' job to go out and find a tree for our living room. The y would always tell me that they worked for it by cleaning the lot or help unloading the trees. But I would not put it past them if they stole one or two of them in the past. There was a time when the kids used to go down to Chubby and Tubby's to get a Christmas tree. The kids would wait until closing time on Christmas Eve, when they almost give the trees away just to get them off their property. To decorate the tree we used to make Christmas tree ornaments out of paper or what ever we could get our hands on. We used to string popcorn and craned berries to wrap around the tree several times. I would make sure they all had something under the tree. I could see in their eyes the hurt, but all I could say was "you just make-do with these". I know that they didn't feel right.

I remember it was just before Christmas and my son Richard was buying gifts from the money he made doing odd jobs around the neighborhood. He had a few extra dollars so he went out bought himself a great big bag of candy. We're from a big family and coming in the house with candy every one would want some of it, so you don't let anybody know you have candy in the bag. So he was sneaking in this bag of candy and I asked him what was in the bag and he said, "nothing" and I said "don't tell me that" and I grabbed the bag and broke a candy bar and all a sudden it struck me and I said, "that wasn't a Christmas gift I just broke was it, I'm sorry" so I let him go up stairs with a bag of candy. He never told me until years later that he thought it was so funny. I went through years thinking that I had broken a Christmas gift.

I remember another Christmas when all the kids always wanted new bikes so I finally found some church to give them to the kids. The bikes were not new but at least they had bikes. We had only two bikes and five kids who wanted to ride. So we spent a lot of time arguing over whose turn it was it ride the bikes. None of them knew how to ride a bike but all of them wanted to learn. They had no one to teach them but they finally figured it out. There was one draw back with these bikes, they were made for adults and the kids were too small to mount the adult size bikes properly. What they did was to stand with the bike between two cars, and getting up on the bike and pushing off from the bumpers of the cars to get moving. I know it was really inconvenient to learn to ride a bike that way because you had to find two cars close enough together that they could get the bike in between them and sometimes they would have to walk a block to find two cars close enough together.

One year Richard bought me a planter that looks like a big wheel for making yarn. He went to the lady up the street and asked her how much it was and he made payments on it to get it for me. Then there was Tim who packed a great big box for Richard. It was 4 feet across and about 3 feet high. It was one box inside a box inside another box inside another box until the box got about the size of a hand and in the last box there was a candy bar. We did have some good times as a family.

Since I lost my oldest son it was my oldest daughters turn to help manage the family. The kids would lie about my oldest daughter Julie just to get her in trouble, because she was the one who was in charge and laid down the rules and made sure the other kids followed them when I wasn't there. They were supposed to do their homework and go to bed at a certain time. I thought that I was tough with the kids but come to find out that Julie was a tyrant. She had that "you do it or your in trouble" state of mind. She popped Tim across the head a couple of times because he was the hardhead of the kids. Robert never did fight with either one of the girls.

They would shake up pop and spray each other with it or take the water hose spray each other with it or fill a cup with water or if the revenge was real bad then it would be a pot of water and dump it on each other.

My brother and sister moved in to the bay area and they would come visiting every month or two. When they did come to visit my brother would always bring food to eat, two main courses with all of the trimmings and the kids would go crazy and stuff them selves. After every body had their fill of food my brother would sit with the kids and tell them ghost stories.

As the years went by the bikes broke down and that was where I told Tim to, "Make a bike with the pieces from both of the bikes." And he did. He was so proud of him self, he made bikes for every one. They found parts from other broken down bikes around the neighborhood. One bike was made from four or five different bikes and they just kept collecting broken bikes to make complete bikes. All of the kids soon had their own bikes and boy it was hard to keep track of where they were then. I swear, it seemed like the way they rode those bikes, in an hour or two they could be in any city in the bay area.

My son Tim used to go two houses down from where we lived to hang out with a guy named Cecil who was a TV repair man. That's when Tim got his first TV. He was so proud of him self. Tim started working for Cecil because Tim showed an interest in electronics and so my son started learning how to fix TV's. Tim's first paycheck was actually a TV for the bedroom he shared. And we didn't' have an outside antenna. He had a hard time getting good reception from the local TV channels. Tim took the TV apart and he could not find the problem. He would take it back to Cecil's and he'd have to go through it again and check everything out and it worked fine at his place with the regular antennae. Every time he said it wasn't' working right. Then he'd have to take it back and Cecil would make him go through it only to find nothing wrong with it and then he would bring it home and it still wouldn't work right. And for the longest time it didn't dawn on him that it was because of the antennae. He made a make shift antenna which was just a wire, which worked.

My son Richard used to mow lawns in the neighborhood. A neighbor named Lew had a strange lawn it was all clover. Lew would spend hours and hours out there doing his yard and garden. He had flowers all over the place with two lemon trees in his back yard, which the kids used to raid. I used to hear them talk about how they pull these commando raids on his lemon trees. They would sneak over and get the lemons. My son told me that after getting the lemons he would jump over the fence he would look and see Lew sitting next to a window inside his house laughing. It was the biggest kick for Lew to watch them go over and steal lemons. My boys really thought they were getting away with something. My boy Tim believed that the lemons were oranges and he could not figure it out because they were so bitter. Once he was corrected, he said, "But they were big ole monster lemons." This was true; they were the size of oranges.

Then there was a guy down the street named Chuck and all the kids in the neighborhood used to go over to Chucks. The kids built a club house in his back yard. Chuck would teach them all how to play football or baseball or swimming and the best thing he taught all of the kids who were neighbors how to get along. There were times when the kids didn't get along and if there was anger between the two he would literally pull them aside to reason out their differences. If that did not work Chuck would set a date and every body would be at his place to watch the fight. Chuck put the gloves on the two guys and let them go at it. Chuck would sit there and coach both of them. He ended up solving a lot of the problems by letting the kids actually fight it out. No one actually got hurt fighting it out.

Chuck wanted to teach all of the sports and he used his back yard for letting the kids practice the high jumping or whatever. I remember my son Richard telling me about the first time he ever tried high jumping. Chuck was pushing my son in that sport because he was better than anyone else at it. My son used to try and dive going across it and Chuck would say, "You can't do that, you have to go over feet first, you can't go over head first." My son tried his best incorporating a side dive over the bar and he started getting his feet to go over at the same time my head went over basically side ways but he was still diving. Chuck insisted that he can't do that and with my son having a hard head kept doing it. It drove Chuck crazy and he would get so upset with that because that was not the rules. Several years later they changed the rules on high jumping where you could actually dive over it. As long as when you dive over you went over sideways.

My son Richard built his first crystal radio set over there at Chucks. He brought it home and set it up in the bedroom. He ran wires for the antenna all over the inside of the bedroom and I wouldn't say anything about stuff like that because they had so little in the first place and he was so proud. We were able to listen to the radio broad cast that we got through the crystal set. A crystal set is a radio that doesn't have a battery. It is a tube or a piece of wood that you wrap a copper wire around it and hook it to a couple of crystals and you had a little move bar that you grabbed down this coil and changed the channel one after another and you could pick up the radio reception with it. I do not know what type of crystals they were. But I do know that you did not have to apply power to it. I'm surprised it's not on the market today.

It's probably not on the market today because you don't have to apply power to it and they only want to have things that you have to apply power to. Everybody had them in the neighborhood. Chuck would let anyone make a crystal set. Everybody in the neighborhood worshiped him. He was like the neighborhood boys club. All the kids went there; he'd take them to movies. He had one son and he had three daughters, and all the boys that he was helping avoided his girls because he was real protective of them. Besides most of the kids were too young for them, but I remember they were real beautiful. That type of person that you don't meet that often anymore.

I took the kids to the beach on a very nice day. We had potato salad, fruit and water to eat and drink. Everybody was having fun playing in the sand, playing tag and jumping the waves. I could not help hearing some white people talking as they walked by. They were calling us "white trash and nigger lovers". Then one lady sent her son to call the sheriff. She thought that just because I had black children I had to be a whore and she did not like the way that their men were looking at me. I knew that if the sheriff stopped me he could drum up something to maybe take my kids away. So we left the beach before he came.

One day one of my children got in a fight with a gang of kids because they threatened the girls. So I called the police because they were much older then my kids. Once the police arrived at our home they asked about the fight and decided kids will be kids and on their way out they noticed my two black kids. They ask who do the kids belong to and I said "me". The police man said, "Don't you ever call the police again and if you do some body is going to jail". After that night I knew it was time to move, just because of the two youngest being black.

By the time we moved to our fourth home in the bay area it seemed like I owed every body in California, from L.A. to the bay area. Thanks to my god given gift of gab I was able to sweet talk a lot of the bill collectors throughout these hard times.

Times were so hard I had to go back to writing bad checks to make ends meet. I wrote a lot of checks. Back in those days you could get an account with a local store and then try and pay it at the end of the month just to keep food on the table. Occasionally the bill got a little bigger than I it wanted to and then I would have a hard time trying to pay it off. My checks weren't that large and all of a sudden I would go down there to pay it and my whole welfare check wouldn't cover it. My line of credit would stop until it was paid off. I would leave an outstanding bill at a store and open another account at a different store. After a while it got really bad. I started sending my kids to the door when ever a bill collector came by, but we didn't have too many people beating on our door about it.

The kids learned at an early stage of their life to keep their money to themselves because I would borrow it and never give it back. Robert had paper route and when he was collecting money he would leave it with me for safe keeping. One day we needed food and before he could turn the money in to the newspaper I borrowed it and spent it on whatever we needed. When it came time to pay the money back I didn't have it, and unfortunately he lost his paper route because of it.

I was used and abused trying to find a good man to help me raise my children. I guess that I like them bad boys because every good man I came across I played one way or the other or subconsciously drove them away.

CHAPTER 6

The Move to Seattle

I REMEMBER THE train ride up here to the Seattle area. I stayed up all night. All of the kids fell to sleep except Tim, who was so excited about the trip. His face was pressed up against the window looking out and he had to tell me every thing he saw going by outside. I was amazed that he was able to see that well out there at night time and after a while I realized that he was making some of that up. He would not stop and in the wee hours of the morning he was driving me crazy with his face up against the window. It seemed like from when we left on the train in California until we arrived up on Seattle. That boy had his face up against that window and looking at everything going by.

The biggest building in town was the Smith Tower Building. It was a huge white tower that stood out on the city skyline. A person could not miss it when you walked out of the train station. All of the buildings around it were small compared to it. Now it is surrounded by sky scrapers and it looks small compared to the buildings around it. Now in these days you would have to look hard to see it. I remember when Ivar's bought the Smith Tower and took down the American flag and put up a huge flag in the shape of a fish. You should have seen the big fuss the city made about it and they made all kinds of treats. Mr. Ivar held his ground and kept his flag up there. We moved up here to Seattle about nine months before the worlds fair happened here. They were still showing the space needle on TV going up in phases advancing a little more and more each day to the completion of the space needle.

The day we got here we all were very hungry and I decided that we were all going to a restaurant to eat. We walked to this little restaurant across the street from the train station called Mom's Café, which is actually this café we are in right now. We had the spaghetti dinner and it was as much as you could eat. The plate would get empty and the lady, Miss Johnston, who was cooking, would put more spaghetti on it. The kids had to tell her that they did not want any more because you had to clean your plate before you left. The kids thought it was a strange restaurant because this café looked more like a home rather than a restaurant.

I was lucky and held a conversation with the Miss Johnston, who owned the café. After hearing about us she decided to be a blessing. She told me don't make no big deal about money, the money wasn't what was important, the important thing was that everybody was full and everybody ate all they could eat free of charge. I spent more time talking to the lady than I spent eating. Somehow there was some kind of vibration that Miss Johnston and I made when I walked in there with all of the kids. Miss Johnson treated all of my kids like they was her kids and she is a real sweet lady and a real good cook too. All of the kids loved being here.

I would take the kids and go down to different restaurants so that the kids would have a chance to see the city and experience dinning in public. Lord knows we could not afford it but I felt it was needed. I know I was a pain to go eat with in a restaurant because they would go ahead and order whatever it was you wanted to have and by the time you were they eating I was just smelling the food and just barely started eating. I remember eating with the kids and as everybody was done eating, I would be there eating. I would be taking these real slow bites and they couldn't get me to speed up because I was enjoying each and every bite. Oh, they got restless. I guess it was my way of teaching them that you're not supposed to eat fast because it gives you indigestion

DAVID DAWN

and you really enjoy the food more when you eat it slowly. I know the kids never wanted to hear that because they just wanted to eat and get it over with.

We used to go to buffet restaurants where you would pick out what you wanted. I used to go to these restaurants and I guess you can say that I started getting carried away because I loved food.

I used to have this thing about food, liked butter, and it used to drive the kids crazy. I would buy a cube of butter and nibble off the cube and wind up eating the whole cube of butter. I loved the taste of butter. I had butter all the time. I would go and get hamburger and put it in the icebox and we'd go in there and grab a piece of hamburger. That is probably where I got the kids in to eating raw hamburger from. One time I had got some sausage, and the kids couldn't tell the difference between hamburger and sausage, and so they were nibbling on the sausage.

I had to teach them that it was wrong and I was telling them about all these worms and how sausage was created. I think I scared them because they could picture these big ole worms crawling around inside of them self and they were all terrorized from any kind of raw meat after that for a while. I had some strange stories I come up with such as that worms grew to be 20 feet long. Today if you eat raw meat you get ecoli because of the deregulation and lack of inspectors in the meat industry. Here I go again straying from the story.

Miss Johnston had a friend who was a real estate agent and she said that he could help me get a house. The real estate agent took us up to a motel. Everyday the real estate agent would come and pick up me and take me around and show me house. He kept taking me and some of the kids every day until we found a house. He was so nice and helpful. I had six kids and staying up in hotel rooms. The boys lost all of their marbles down the storm drain of the motel parking lot. After of about a week of looking for a house that fit our needs and income we found a 4 bedroom with a basement. It was a true blessing. One of my boys complained all day for several days because he had to sleep at the end of the fold out couch that folded out in to a bed and for some reason he was always chosen to sleep along the bottom of the bed. If not one kid was kicking him the other one was he caught all the feet. Everybody during the night kicked me at least once a night. Keep in mind that it did not help the sleeping arrangement when some body is tickling feet half the night.

Again I found all of the welfare money went to paying the rent so I rented out the basement which had several rooms in it. I was lucky to start a food account at the local store that had a manager that was so nice. I was lucky for the local churches and charity organizations because they help furnish the house. Every thing was used and some of it was pretty worn out and nothing matches but we put it all too good use.

I found a job as a cook at a frat house. I was a pretty good cook but at home we had very little to cook with so the kids were never happy with my food. The kids were very under standing they knew it was because of the money situation. I did not last long on the job due to the varicose veins in my legs. All of that standing just inflamed them.

The kids got so they hated biscuits and cornmeal patties. My son Robert ate so much peanut butter that it made him so sick he couldn't eat peanut butter for a long time. Another son of mine does not like mayonnaise to this day because there was a time when we had to rotate between cornmeal and potatoes with mayonnaise to eat for weeks. So, one morning we were having potatoes and mayonnaise for breakfast and he through up all over the table. I think I added a bit too much mayonnaise. Tim ended up hating potatoes and the girls hated corn meal mush. We would take the little red wagon up to the local store and buy bags of potatoes and beans in the 100lb bags and then we used to buy mayonnaise by the gallon jars. They all got tired of eating dull food. But at the time you know when you are feeding a mob like that you got to make it last a while. You got to buy in bulk. You got to buy what you can. It was interesting.

One Valentines Day my daughter Julie tried to cook breakfast for me, it was her first time cooking. My kitchen was turned into a disaster area. The entire kitchen was a mess. There were burnt pans, flour and grease every where. She tried to make eggs which she burnt. She tried to make sausages and some were burnt and others weren't even cooked. And then she tried to make pancakes and it turned out to be a regular cake because she kept adding all these ingredients and pretty soon I ended up with a big ole round cake. She had worked so hard to make me happy. All I could think of was "Bless her soul" and I sat there and ate a little bit of every thing. As she stood there watching, I had to tell her how good it was.

I remember Robert went out and bought one of these nice heavy sweaters at the time, it was in style at the time. He bought it with his paper route money. I got cold one night, put it on and really stretched it out. It never did fit him after that. He was so sad about it that he gave it to me and said, "It's yours I don't want it back. You can keep it mom, it'll never fit me the same." I felt soooo, bad.

My girls were wearing shoes that were too small for them and they always had to share the clothes. For over a year they had only one nice dress to share for going out on dates.

The first time my kids saw snow they ran out in their P.J.'s and played in the snow until they were wet from head to toe. After coming in and changing in to their warm clothes they went back out and played all day in it.

The kids would sneak down and sit on the stairs and watch TV after they were supposed to be in bed. That worked for a while until they got caught because of someone making noise.

My two black sons walked all the way down to the world's fair and back home. They told us about how they got kicked out of the Shell gas station. People would toss coins into the pools and they would go in there and steal the nickels, dimes, and quarters. They went back several times until they got caught.

Tim and his friend used to sneak in to the science center. It was their favorite place because there was so much to learn in the science center. They went in there in the middle of the night, and the place wasn't even open. They enjoyed on all the different scientific things in there. The best exhibit he liked was the one where you're walking up hill but it feels like you're walking down hill.

At this stage of life everyone was growing up so fast. All of my white kids were at least in their mid teens. Their needs had grown just as they did. It was a blessing that the kids did help out in their own ways to help keep food on the table and a sense of family values.

We were always getting handouts from the state and local churches. I would try to repay the churches generosity by volunteering my services as a cook. When they would have the banquets I would always help cook the meals. Afterwards it was feast time for my family, as I would always bring home leftovers. They would have roast beef, mashed potatoes, dinner rolls, and all the fixings for a good meal. We would sit home and eat like fat pigs. You could see the contentment on their faces. Everyone was full and happy. It was like Thank giving all over again.

My youngest daughter Sue worked for A&W and she used to bring home fries and stuff. The kids would stay up late knowing that Sue was going to bring home hamburgers and french-fries. Every once in a while she would bring home root beer floats.

The kids in the neighborhood had a little deal going on because they needed enough kids to play foot ball. The kids would stand outside the house and play on the porch and in the yard making all kinds of noise and you would shoo them away and they would come back doing the same thing until that child could come out to play. The kids would stand outside the house and chant, "we want in, we want in." until the parents let their kid go out and play. They thought that was so cool. It got to the point that I got so tired of them I would let the kids go out and play with them to get them to shut up. It even worked if the kid was on restriction or had chores to do that would end real quickly when the kids would stand out there chanting. I was not the only parent to fall victim to this, all of the neighborhood parents did.

A lot of times the kids would play hide and seek and they had a hiding limit of five houses in either direction. They could only use the front yard, the back yards were off limits. Robert, being a fast runner, would wait until the "seeker" got a ways away from the base. He would start in a full run and by the time the "seeker" realized that Robert was running to the base it was too late to catch him.

Tim was always fighting with everybody and I was in poor health, trying to go out and earn a living. When I would get home there was all this tension in the house because the hard times was taking its toll. Four of them were teenagers with their own minds. All of them was a know it all.

This was the time when the children was starting to move out, one by one as the years went by until I was left with the two little boys. There was a gap in the ages between the white children and the black children by five years. I felt that the two boys needed to be with their own race because they had been living in white neighborhoods most of their lives. There is a difference of how the two races look at life due to society's rules. So I felt it would do them good. We moved to the south side of Seattle in the projects. There was a good mixture of races there. Every one had their own room and that was a 1st for the boys. I had come to find out that the kids was being treated the same as the white kids in school with the teasing of their mother being white. I had the label of white trash once more. As time went on the kids were accepted by everyone.

I started slowly losing control of my kids. This was due to not being strict with them and I almost always let them do what they wanted. Well to make a long story short I lost my two boys. The authorities came and took them away. I had to change my name again to prevent the law from arresting me for writing bad checks. It was a time of great turmoil in all of our lives. I knew that I had to become a better example for my kids. I know that I should have done it a long time ago.

CHAPTER # 7

The Golden Years

AFTER ALL THE kids moved out I moved in to the senior citizens apartments on Yester Ave. which was on the edge of China Town. I had become the apartment Manager at night. I also clean the side walks for business in the China Town area for extra money and restaurant credit.

One day we had a picnic for the old folks there and there was a kind of steep incline for a short distance. I started walking down it when I lost my footing and then I lost my balance. The next thing I knew was that I was head over heals and bounced up and landed on my feet. Everybody sat there and didn't know what to say but when I landed on her feet everybody applauded. Now that was a once in a life time event. Some one was really looking out for me.

I had the gift of bargaining. I remember we used to go to china town and we'd get free food and I used to run up the bill and I used to make payments to the owner of the restaurant for the food we ate prior. I started the first Christmas meal for the homeless in China Town. I went down and got people to volunteer their building for that cause. Then I went to store owners and got them to contribute all the food and drinks. It was so successful that other people got involved in it and did it for the next couple of Christmas's.

I have another story to tell. This one is a hum dinger. It is sort of a shocker to me. I will try to be abrupt and to the point. I went to the Social Security Office reporting that I had a job and that I was not sure that I could handle it, but I'd like to try. I know that I have the ability, so it all depended on my health and I wondered if the men would accept a woman being apartment manager.

I was put in complete charge of the apartments during the day shifts, for Saturday and Sundays only. In that building and in that neighborhood anything and everything could happen and usually does. I liked working for the owners; they were fair people with good hearts. The tenants were glad to see me. The owner slipped and said that I was a strong woman. He rarely says what he thinks about me.

The only things happening around the apartments, were like, a water leak from upstairs which ran down in to the Japanese restaurant cocktail lounge below and I have to go find who's sink or tub is over running or a street walker is trying to get in the building to knock on the doors, which is a no, no. I am responsible for the security of the building, which has 6 different entrances and the office is at the front main door. Then there are characters like poor Chuck, who stood 6 feet tall. When he is sober, which is rarely, he can barely talk. So in his stupor, he still comes and tries to sneak in to the apartments because he was put out a year and a half ago, as a tenant. Once he is in the building, he will lie down or should I say, rather he falls down and he's so hard to get up. Then a woman tenant will see a man in the hallway and will come to the office, complaining, there is a man lying on the floor next to the elevator and I am afraid to pass him to get to my apartment. An outsider comes in to visit a friend and then they cannot find their way out of the 11 story building. This is the type of things that happen often when I am working on the weekend. Golly! Some of these men are big, husky and rough individuals. May God bless them all. There were a lot of times when I had to call the Aid Car and they would some times call De-Tox wagon.

One night a couple of tenants complained of a strong offensive odor. Upon checking it out, my passkey did open this door, but he had a strong door chain that was latched on the inside. I went down to the lobby to look around for someone to help. Sitting in a lobby chair and

I saw a man looking out of the window. I said to myself, now there is a strong man, who, I hope he is not too emotional, because his arm was in a cast and he will have a foot operation in a few weeks. I looked around and I could not see anyone as strong as he, so here it goes. I ask him, I am in need a strong shoulder. I asked him if he was curious and he said, yes, so I asked him to come along with me.

On the elevator, where no other tenant could hear, I ask him if he could bust in a door. He said, sure as long as I have your O.K., I am a retired prison guard. The gent, who came to help with the door, only had to bust two screws off the wall, which held the chain on. For when I used my pass key to reopen the door, we knew the odor was a man who had been dead for at least two weeks. His windows were closed and the maggots were all ready started. The Coroner had a mask over his nose. I wish that I had a mask too, because that evening at home I still had the odor in my nose hairs. I would breathe out strongly and rub my nose as a dog would with his paw, as a dog would after he smelt some thing strong, trying to get rid of the strong smell, Gees!

I could go on and on about tenant stories, but I had better get back to my own story. Where I am living, here in China Town, the apartment manager gave me an eviction notice or should I say 3 of them. The first notice was a 3 day notice. She must have been in a hurry at that time because shortly after I received 2 other notices claiming that I had 30 days to move. Here the apartment manger and I had been working for the same bosses or apartment owners. I have been a tenant in these apartments for over 8 years. I do not come in to the apartments drunk, I do not bother my neighbors and it just does not make any sense. Of course the unwritten truth is that the tenants asked me to come on the Residence Council and they voted me to be the Vice President. I am also the Second Vice President of the Pike Place Market Senior Community Center. I became the Liaison Person between the Resident Council and the Senior Board of Directors and as an extra little job to fix my problem I am on the Executive Committee and the Personal Committee. Anyway to get back to the eviction, which was the underlying reason. If I was to get evicted from the building, I automatically would not and could not be on the Resident Council. But I do not want to give up my apartment just yet and the choice should be mine.

My kids would come and visit me once in a while and I would keep them up to speed with what is happening in my life. My dear Richard says, " Do not give up, give them a fight and give them all that you have to give". I guess that this old lady can make a good strong stand, especially if my sons say so. My dear Kain says, "Do not give up, I am proud of you mom, for standing your ground". This eviction deal is highly undignified. I do not deserve this type of treatment from the manager of the apartments, who is acting under the advisement of people I will not name, who is opposed to the politic goals of the committees that I work with.

I had offered to pay my rent in advance for June. The manager refused the rent money and she had proper grounds, for I needed to be recertified, because of the change of income. So, I, in the next few days got the statements that where needed from the Social Security Office and the owners of the apartments and thus, gave all of the paper work to the manager of the apartments. During this time the apartment manager refused to take my rent and this continued in to July. On July 5, I again offered to pay the rent, with cash in hand for the months of June and July. This will make 5 times I had tried to pay my rent, but was refused acceptance of rent monies. Yet, I was accused of being behind on my rent, Geese! It was the apartment manager's doings that had put me behind on the rent. So I put the money in to the bank for safe keeping. I was to be evicted on the 5 of August. I was tired of fighting like heck to do the right thing, so I went above the apartment manager's head. I think that being a good tenant for over 8 years should have a little play in what happens to me as well as the work that I have done for the owners and the residents of the two apartments. On top of that the apartment manager has the nerve to say, between the uses, being owners and committees. She has been a good bed buddy and she loves to play politics.

Anyway, on August 3, I went to the owner's office and met with the owners Business Manager. I had told him that the money is piling up in the bank and my rent still is not paid. I did not say to the Business Manager that they are short on bank funds to make their mortgage payments, as I had learned from being on the Board of Directors. The Business Manager and owners knew of my efforts with the tenants, community and apartment affairs and they had always liked what they had seen, so the Business Manager said, O.K., Betty, you just bring in the money, because we really need it and I will give you a receipt for the rent. I wrote out a personal check right there and then stating that it was for June, July and this month August. The manager of the apartments sent me a receipt for the 3 months, with a notice claiming that I still might be evicted at the end of the month anyway. Geeeeesse what a witch. They should know the letters of the laws better, being a manager. If they want to play cat and mouse, they had better be good, because I hate the game. A game I much detest.

If they try to evict me in September they have to legally start all over again, with a 30 day notice, which I will refuse to accept, which means court action and that takes a week or two. I would rather have a Court Judge say that I am undesirable, if that can be said or proven. Through court each eviction cost two hundred dollars for the process. The management can not afford the cost, for there are others that she wants out. Also the apartment manager has accused me of a criminal action of Section1001 for misrepresenting, but she does not say what. But I know she means monies. I went to the Social Security Office in May and in the last week of July reporting my change of income each time it had changed. I do not have to report to her and she figures that I did not make the reports.

I have worked for two months. My legs and hips are hurting and at times cramping very badly. That is why I can not keep working at the apartments. As for now only my right leg is hurting. During the night, while I sleep, I get tired of sleeping on my back and turn to one side. I need to be sure that I do not stay much longer then 3 to5 minutes or for sure I will start cramping very bad on that leg. When I was working at the apartments, the desk chair set crooked, which tends to throw my body frame out of line. The shifts lasted for 12 hours on the weekend.

I took a trip to see my oldest son Paul in L.A. and when I had gotten back the apartment manager had given away all of my personal belongings that I had in a storage room, located in the basement of the building. She told the tenants that they could help them self's and that I was giving away my belongings. This was very untrue! I should sue her for that action, because she will do it to the next tenant who stands up to her. The charge of Defamation of Character really gets to me. If they are not stopped they will trump up other ungrounded charges against me, just to make sure that they get their way. All my life I have been against suing, but now I am certainly thinking about it.

Ever so often, I feel like leaving Seattle, because I do not like fighting. I have had too much of it in my life. Golly, some times a person will look at me, when I am in a pleasant mood and smiling and they will say, "You must have had a good life, meaning a good and easy going life." I am not one who goes around crying the blues, I do not believe in doing that. Often I wonder if I should live in Janesville, Madison or Milwaukee. I would not give it a second thought of leaving Seattle, except for it being so far away from my 4 sons.

Dearest Richard and my dearest youngest son Mark keep asking me when am I going to move in to their houses in Lynnwood, but it is about 15 miles back in to Seattle and I love and enjoy the country life still, because it is so peaceful. Yet, I know that I would soon miss the hussel and bussel of the big city.

All of this tension is not helping my arthritis. I ended up moving deeper in to China Town. Of course being the Vice President of the Residence Council, the Second Vice President of the Pike Place Market Senior Community Center, the Liaison Person between the Resident Council and the Senior Board of Directors and I am on the Executive Committee and the Personal Committee and this had leaded me to also be on the advisor for the China Town Community Board I took on projects to keep it looking beautiful, like cleaning empty lots of its trash in my spare time. I would go around with the yellow raincoat on and with a broom and dustpan and sweep the sidewalks of these stores and wash the windows. This is how I would make ends meet. I got free meals and pay from the store owners.

I didn't get to see much of the kids after the moved to china town. I guess they were off living their own life's, creating their own families and working hard to do things right in our mixed up society.

When I moved to china town it was in a part that if you weren't Chinese it wasn't safe to be in china town after dusk because you could get beat up by anybody. I'm referring to the teenage gangsters, druggies, drunks or just your every-day person who was down and out. But everybody who lived around there knew and liked me. Down at the bottom of my apartment there was a marshal arts school and the instructor there who became my friend. Whenever my kids come to visit me and someone would start harassing us the instructor of the school would come out and everyone would be scared of him. He would stand up for us and after while no one would bother me or my kids because of him. A couple of times he threatened to beat some of the gang bangers. After a while we were known as friends of his friends and no one would mess with us. Through my positive attitude towards everyone around me would just draw themselves to help me all the time. I don't know how I did it but inevitably wherever we moved there would be people around me that would watch out for me and my kids.

Back in Chinatown there was this park that I was cleaning up, and was picking up all the beer bottles and wine bottles out there and everything with the yellow raincoat washing. I remember telling him that I started on my own to clean it up project. It was a project to keep all of the vacant lots clean from all the trash the homeless would leave behind and I mowed what little grass that there was. The merchants really appreciated the effort I had put in on this project.

I contacted the people of Hong Kong and talked them into donating an oriental gazebo. I got the people there in Chinatown to go out there mow the grass and pick up the garbage. There was a corner lot in the heart of Chinatown where the drunks and others hung around that I thought would be perfect for the oriental gazebo.

I got the city council and the community board to change one of the lots in to a park. This was my project and it made me feel very good about my self. It was something I could show my kids and inspire them to do good things too. I was surprise to see all of the neighborhood support on the project.

I wrote a letter to arrange for Hong Kong to donate that shrine and to redo the grounds there. Not only did Hong Kong donate the whole building and all the art work with it but also all the bricks that was laid on the ground and the labor to assemble it. So I arranged for them to pay for all of it.

The ship pulled into the harbor and trucks were loaded up with all the parts for this new park and they were moving it over to the site. The Mayor shows up with a gold shovel to break the ground, he knew nothing about it until he was notified that all this stuff was being moved over there. It was an election year and he showed up there with all this press and this gold shovel to take pictures of him breaking the ground and him telling this big story about how he's had this secret about something he wanted to do for Chinatown and in reality it had nothing to do with him. He didn't find out about it until half and hour before that. Just long enough to get the gold shovel and run down there to take the credit for it and get the press down there.

After the park was made and the beautiful shrine came from China the city had a big fan-fair over it. I had gotten very little credit for the park. The Mayor gave a speech about building up the trade with China and how this will strengthen the bond of friendship between the two. The papers gave him all the credit even though I did all of the leg work to pull it together. He did not even mention me or say thanks and the Chinese businessmen were really mad about it.

There is a big plaque in there and I was down there looking at it not too long ago. It had a list of all these people involved with the construction of this thing and upgrading in Chinatown. My name is not on the plaque and the names on there had nothing to do with it. Everybody took credit for what I and the Chinese businessmen did. To myself I got mad, I got furious when I saw this big ole' plaque of all these names. Gee politicians can be so greedy at any level of government.

I started another project and it was the first Christmas meal for the homeless. I went down and got these people to volunteer their building for that cause. Then I went to store owners and got them to contribute all the food and I talked everyone into donating everything. I put on the first Christmas meal for the homeless down there. Then that took off and other people got involved in it and again I was never given any credit for the meals that I set up in Chinatown for the homeless which now they do once a year at the Christmas celebration. I got that started and again I get no credit maybe it is because of the things I did in the past. Lord knows, I am telling you the nicer side of the life and what my family had gone through. Maybe this is pay back for all the wrong things that I had done.

I was the only woman that had pictures of me sitting at the china counsel table. In the history of Chinatown there has never been any woman allowed to sit at the china town counsel and this was during the counsel meeting. It was only to show how much respect that they had for me and the work that I had done in the community. It was only a one time thing but no woman white or Chinese has ever sat at a counsel meeting table and it was in the news paper too. For them to even let me in the room was amazing. I am good friends with Ruby Chow who was on the city counsel for a long time. Do you remember that movie of Bruce Lee's life and him washing dishes? When it comes time for him to leave the owner of the restaurant ask him if he wants to go to college or be a dish washer for the rest of his life? Well as a matter of fact that lady was Ruby. She had a way of bring the best out of people without even trying.

I had to give my son Tim a birthday party. It was down in Chinatown and at the best Chinese restaurant in the city. Year after year they were classified as the best Chinese restaurant and it happen to be Ruby's. They closed off the restaurant and no one was allowed in there except the people in the birthday party even though big -wigs were standing in line for a table. I finally realized what was happening and I told them you go open up that part over there which they did and let high paying customers come in.

I was called to the counter and the waiter was saying that I have to pay now and the bill was tremendous. I was trying to tell the cashier that she had made arrangements with the owner on the bill. This guy was raising hell with me. Ruby heard the loud speaking man and came out to see what was going on. The cashier told her that the lady will not pay her bill. She spoke to him in their language and the guy shut up and looked at me and looked back at Ruby and then she took the bill and ripped it up and threw it in the garbage. She told me to go back in there and finish enjoying my family.

I helped the China town business community to upgraded china town and with the help of Ruby who was on the city counsel and the business owners we made it safe for visitors to be in China town. I did not get credit for the shrine or the park and not even with the Christmas dinners for the homeless but I was shown the real appreciation and gratitude for the things that I did for the Chinatown community and the upgrading in the Chinatown business area to make it a cleaner and safer for people to be in Chinatown. The way the business and the leaders of the community treated me was the greatest reward of all.

To top it all off, some time went by and the local paper needed some elderly woman in their advertisement. They interviewed hundreds and they picked me. So, my picture with a motor cycle helmet on was plastered all over the city. Some of the ads read, "You can sell anything in the paper" and others said "I sold my motor cycle in the want ads." I was on buses, billboards, and taxis. One of my sons almost got in a car crash when he saw me on the billboard as he stopped in the middle of traffic and just starred at the billboard. Another son was in the car describing me to his new girlfriend and all of a sudden she says, "No, no you're not describing your mom your describing the lady on the bus" and he turned and looked, and there's my picture, on the side of the bus.

There is a company who wants me to be a spokesman for them, but I am going to pass because this old body of mine is completely worn out. I am lucky that I made it to the café today. I was told by a doctor that I had terminal cancer that is running all through my body. He told me, if I was lucky, I might live for six more months. Here I am 27 years after that. I guess that I am just too god damn stubborn to lay down and die. I am really feeling it now. I guess you can say that I have been living on borrowed time.

I hurt all over, so I went to the doctor yesterday and gosh, I was there half of the day. Finally the doctor came back to me and said that he wanted to admit me into the hospital. Right away I said, "No you people will kill me." The doctor said, "Betty we don't even know how come you are still alive. All of your body is eat'n up from cancer except for your brain. One of your lungs is almost totally gone, and the other one was three quarters the way gone". By all rights I shouldn't have even been alive according to modern day medicine. Lord knows, I should have been dead along time ago.

With that being said I looked at Sue and said, "Well, young lady I told you my life story and I must say that telling you it has brought back so many good memories, as will as bad ones. I know that I wore your ear out but I truly believe that I lived this long just to meet you and hopefully shed some wisdom on the life you might have ahead of you. It all depends on the decisions you make when you come to the many different crossroads of life. Do not be a fool for men who do not have their act together or run away the good ones, like I did. That action by it self will make a big difference in your life and the lives of your children." Being Little Miss. Know it all was the reason why I did not choose the right men or raise my kid's right.

Decades of studies show that children will be successful in learning through all of the school years when their family shows support for them in every way possible. The main educational source any parent could give their children is reading. Reading to and with your children and have them talk about what has been read. It is very important that they understand what is being read. You need to help them with their homework. If you do not know how to help with the homework, then talk to them about how they can get help with their homework. Follow through and check on the type of help you two decided on and have them teach you some things about their homework to make sure that they know what they are talking about. Talk with their teachers and the parents of their friends and take part in their school and youth activities.

By doing this your child will have a great advantage in learning and will be far ahead of those children who do not get the love, attention, support, and wisdom that every parent is suppose to give their children. They will have the knowledge of how a family works as a team and the wisdom of running a family. If the parent shows the value and the enjoyment in reading they will teach their children to be a proud citizen of a hard working community.

Everyone knows that it is three to ten times harder for a single parent to raise children and to keep them unified as a family. For a single parent they will have to sacrifice all of their spare time to maintain the home and the teachings of their children. It is a real 24-7 job. Raising children by your self or even with a mate is hard work because you have to be very repetitious every day in your teachings with the rules, love, attention, support, wisdom and disciplining. By doing this the odds is your child will grow up to be good, well rounded parents, too?

The less time you spend with your children the less a parent repeats them self, the less strict the parents are about following the rules, that are set by the parent. This makes it harder to raise the children and it will lead to the children not listening, being sloppy with their manners, less self respect, less respect for those around them, being embarrass of them self, being withdrawn and shy, which will lead to them living a life of being very defensive, etc., etc., etc. If you raise your children this way, odds are that they will grow up to be bad parents. Thank god my oldest children took control of that.

If you were a child who was embarrassed about your skills and do not improve upon the skills that you are lacking, then, as the time goes by the lack of skills will grow. The next thing you will know or wonder about is, why did you drop out of school or why did you start hanging with those kind of kids? The less that you take part in learning the less successful you will be in life. If some thing is missing in the family structure like love, attention, a parent, discipline, leadership, joy, money etc., etc., etc. then that child might look out side of the family to have that in their life.

The goal of a parent is to unite all the members to be as one happy well rounded family. Our children need us to install and promote pride, happiness, self-improvement, stabilization, harmony, leadership and love in and between all the members of the family. We as individual parents have different techniques in raising our children due to the different life styles and the way we were raised as children. We need to keep open minds to new ideas and techniques as the children grow and change. Keeping the door of communication open will work wonders in running a family. As good parents we must work on changing the negative cycles that has stayed with us and our patents for the good of our own families.

It is time for you to go to the shelter up on 5th Street and see Mr. Wilson he will set you up with every thing that you will need to move on with your life. He will open the door of opportunity for you, but it is up to you to work hard at making a good life for you and your children.

Several weeks went by and the young pregnant girl decided to stop by the café to see Miss Johnston and Betty. Miss Johnston told the girl that after you had left Betty fell ill. Betty has passed on and I believe that talking to you was her last mission in her life.

She was an amazing woman you know, she did a lot of things that are not in the ordinary. It was like she made people feel good about helping her. And so they would go out of their way to help her just so that they could feel a lot better. She used it to help her family, friends and the community. Every place she went it wouldn't take long to make friends either and they would look out for all of the kid's too. She had that charisma. Betty and I got along from the start just like we was friends for life.

Though the years I learn from Betty is once you have a strong sense of self worth it creates the will power to improve your self and it will ripple out to those around you. You need to teach and show your friends the way to develop a strong respectful adult relationship with the opposite sex. You need to teach as well as show your friends the means to change the cycles of all of their negative emotional habits that keep our souls earthbound in a self-created ego prison with the bars molded out of negative thoughts and bad habits. Any limitations that we perceive are only in our minds. Change your thoughts and you change your life in to developing a positive self. This would lead to living a much better life and achieving your goals.

When she died the leader of a church heard that Betty a follower of this church and did a lot of volunteering. We would like to pay respects by planting a rose bush in the rose garden in San Jose for her in her honor. So there is a rose bush in San Jose that is Betty's rose bush.

DAVID DAWN

27196361R20058

Made in the USA
San Bernardino, CA
11 December 2015